THE TWELVE EVEN
STRANGER DAYS OF
CHRISTMAS

THE TWELVE EVEN
STRANGER DAYS OF
CHRISTMAS

SYD MOORE

A Point Blank Book

First published by Point Blank,
an imprint of Oneworld Publications, 2021

ISBN 978-1-78607-979-4
ISBN 978-1-78607-980-0 (ebook)

Oneworld Publications
10 Bloomsbury Street
London WC1B 3SR
England

Stay up to date with the latest books,
special offers, and exclusive content from
Oneworld with our newsletter

Sign up on our website
oneworld-publications.com/point-blank

For Josie and Samuel,
steadfast and true

[definition] Strange /streɪn(d)ʒ/

Adjective: strange
1. Unusual or surprising; difficult to understand or explain.

Comparative adjective: stranger; *superlative adjective:* strangest

Synonyms: Odd, curious, peculiar, funny, bizarre, weird, uncanny, queer, unexpected, unfamiliar, abnormal, atypical, anomalous, different, out of the ordinary, out of the way, extraordinary, remarkable, puzzling, mystifying, mysterious, perplexing, baffling, unaccountable, inexplicable, incongruous, uncommon, irregular, singular, deviant, aberrant, freak, freakish, surreal, alien.

CONTENTS

PANTOMIME

Nobody ever realised that the seven dwarves were female. I suppose it was an easy mistake to make. At the time. Society wasn't as enlightened as it is now, for sure. Not that we haven't got far to go. It still ain't bread and roses. But anyways, when I am feeling benevolent, I can look back and kinda see the confusion, what with us all having those nicknames of ours. But how folks didn't see through that I just don't know. And the way all of them come about, well they weren't what you might think at all. It was gradual like, lots of different situations.

Take Happy: she was one of the first patients to ever trial Valium, way back in the day. But that didn't get her the name. No, her husband, James, had been a brute. She was so overjoyed when he ran off with a long-legged dancer called Dora she was able to ditch the drugs and come to us deep deep deep in the forest. Mining was a walk in the park compared to keeping house for that god-awful thug. Happy, she never forgot the darkness of her life before. Every single day she would get up and count out loud her blessings. We loved her. She kept us bright.

Then there was Sleepy. She had a condition. And, as a group, I'd say we were fair, so there was never any problem with the lie-ins. Everybody needs their beauty sleep. Some more than others. And so, Sleepy paid the favour back by keeping the house and doing the donkey's load of washing. See, each of us had a job to do. Now, Bashful was a nickname for Toots-Louise, a former showgirl. Name-dropped constantly, but there weren't no harm in it. Amused us. Said she'd roomed with Barbara Stanwyk before she made the big screen. Maybe she did, maybe she didn't? Who cared? No one in the woods, that's who. Sneezy soon paired off with Dopey after she arrived. Probly she never really should have lived in a forest with her allergies, but she liked the lifestyle and she was good for D, so we let it go. Though it was fair to say, come summertime, with the constant sniffling and coughing, some tempers frayed. Namely Grumpy's. But she was menopausal so, you know, we made allowances.

A lot of folk were interested in how we managed to afford the house, the acres and live as well as we did. Most knew about the mine but it didn't make as much as they assumed. We had a lucrative sideline in a field not far from the cottage with a very special crop. Dopey took care of that and made enough dough for us not to worry over bills and whatnot. But she sampled the merchandise too often, so you can see where I'm going with her name.

And then there was me, Doc, and of course everyone thought I was a guy.

Of. Course. They. Did.

I wasn't.

Funny that I never really bothered about putting it straight before. But time being of the essence now that I am come to my end, I thought I should probly correct it.

So, there's we were, all living mighty freely and doing our own thing. We'd work with commitment during the day, some down the mine, others in the house, tending the crop or selling our product in the city. Come the evening the flock would return to the nest, like homing pigeons, to feast and sing and play. We worked well, fitted together like some crazy jigsaw – a bunch of women from different places who all washed up on my land for one reason or another. And who made good.

Summers in those deep, dark woods stretched out like a lazy cat. Bashful would make up a barbecue out front – she had worked in a diner previous. Happy liked to serve us her Creole shrimp. We would spend hours out the front porch, those sultry evenings, supping and shooting the breeze. There were four brothers living in the next valley, giants who made mayonnaise and moonshine. I had served with Gabe, the eldest, back in the War. Alliances were made. So, come the sunshine, on occasion those boys would troop over to our place and we'd sing in the midnight hour.

Good days.

Now, it was winter when Whitey made her appearance. The snow was thick on the ground and she was just as pale when she knocked upon our door. Grumpy took her in and, having a literal frame of mind, commented upon her pallor. That's how her nickname come on. Whitey didn't ever want her real name told. Though we got it out of her in the end. Had to really.

From the off I could see that Whitey wasn't like the rest of them. Couldn't put my finger on it, though I was moved by her story. After her real mama died, another broad made moves on her father. And no less than a year after Whitey's momma was in the ground, the girl was presented with a new stepmom. But this lady, she was jealous of Whitey. To be honest, I didn't think Whitey was all that, but the other girls thought she had a prettiness about her that was worth remark. The stepmom, though, she was uncomfortable with her new daughter's looks. Some women are like that, I'm told, with beauty. It unnerves them. Me – I always thought it a curse. The women who've passed through here, they been all types of beautiful, and I ain't seen many that have made it work for them. But back to Whitey. This darned stepmom, well, she turned the girl out. Into the cold. And the father didn't bat an eyelid.

Anyways we tried to make her feel okay, but she was a handful. Had no stamina for work. Kind of thought she was above it. Dopey reckoned our newcomer had a princess complex, thought she was going to be rescued by a knight in shining armour. We'd had some of this type before. But the fact of the matter was that if you didn't work, you couldn't stay. Of course, some women, they had to recover from wherever, whoever and whatever they'd been through, before they could muck in. We were aware that most folk who turned up were running away from something. So we took patience and waited for Whitey's tale to out.

Months passed. She seemed content to walk the meadows picking flowers. It wasn't on the list of chores, but we tried to make with the compliments and hoped she'd bloom out herself. She didn't. So we sent her out to help Dopey with the crop, but she'd just end up tootling around and fall asleep in the fields. One of us would have to pick up the barrow, load her in and bring her back till she woke.

Her being the way she was, we charged Sleepy with organising her. Our domestic manager put her on housekeeping duties. Easy, right? Only problem with that was ole Whitey had this thing about animals. Thought she could parlay with them. I know. One day, when she was meant to be scrubbing out the pantry, Sleepy comes in and only finds all these critters on the counters: rabbits by the sink, chipmunks in the pots licking the scraps, a pair of bluebirds at the window pecking breadcrumbs she'd *put* there, and they was doing their business all over the sill. The very definition of UNSANITARY.

So off she comes from house duties. We thought we'd stick her down the mine for a while. Lasted but a day. Heigh ho.

Bashful says, 'Let her go with me to street sell. She got a real nice face and a friendly manner. If she does well I can take her to the pictures. As a reward.' We thought this over and concurred it might do some good, shake her up a little, help her get back that mojo. If she ever had one.

So offs they go. All zipped up with money in their pockets to get them some luncheon.

We had high hopes.

Only.

Didn't go so well. Not for us anyways.

So it seems for a while Whitey's doing all right. Then up comes this spivvy-looking fella, spins her a line about how pretty she is, and says he's a casting agent uptown. Asks if she can spare a bit of product for some of the big shot stars over there and has she thought about acting or modelling herself? Bashful had been bending her ear to the whole patter and was 'bout to step in but then comes an old contact of hers and asks how the crop's going this year. Well, they be chewing the fat and trying the product and having a nice chunk of good time, so Bashful forgets about her babysitting. Few minutes later, when she looks again, Whitey's disappeared.

So right about this point, Bashful's beside herself. She returns to the roost in a fine old temper, a-cussing and a-downing on herself, worried over Whitey.

As it goes, she shouldn't have.

Whitey turns up later that evening, full of airs, and raving her heart out about how she been to the studios and met some beautiful people. The agent, in particular, she won't stop gassing about – says he's so clever, a Princeton graduate no less, calls him 'a right charmer'. Then she tells us he wants to audition her for a part. And she is so super shined up by this guy's attentions she gives him all of the product.

As you can imagine we was all up in arms.

'Cept it's water off a duck's back. Our words don't even register in Whitey's little brain on account of how she is just going on and on 'bout how this is her big break.

Problem is Happy, who was commonly in charge of the finances, is having none of it. Tells her she has to go back and get payment. Bashful agrees and, I guess cos she's feeling a bit itchy about her part in the fiasco, announces she'll accompany ole Whitey. As I am pretty much queen of this kingdom I tell them that I'll come too. Safety in numbers and all that. Plus I've a pistol which might come in handy should the freeloaders get feisty.

So the next morning Whitey leads us back to the studio which, to both mine and Bashful's surprise, *is* actually a studio. Though they're ten a penny round here, and not always what they says on the tin, but this one looks legit. When we goes in though, there's already a bit of a buzz fizzing up. One of the gals ain't showed to the rehearsal and the producer and her roommate are none too happy. The roommate says her friend, Bertha, had gone to audition for a part in a new movie 'bout a spy girl who goes on missions and uses men like disposable hankies. I quite liked the sound of it, but that weren't the point. The point was she weren't where she was meant to be and it wasn't in her character to be tardy.

Though we hadn't yet announced ourselves and were holding back for a good moment, I could see that Bashful's eyes were narrowing. Something was troubling her.

'What's his name?' she asked. 'The guy who's called the casting?'

And the roommate turns to us '"Victor the Palaeontologist" is what she calls him on account of how he likes to admire her bones.'

And Bashful nods and says, 'I've heard of this wise guy. Some of my old chorus gals have had dealings.

He's a wrong 'un, for sure. Uses a room downtown in the Hotel California.'

So that does it, and within seconds there's us three in the motor alongside the roommate, Sindy, and for some unknown reason, the graduate agent who Whitey's all over and has started calling her own 'Princeton Charming'.

Once we get there, we explain to the duty manager what's going on and there's a girl missing, but he's reluctant to cooperate and I don't feel it right to force the issue with my steel so we go outside to regroup and ponder. But as we're doing that, the receptionist turns up. Now she's got a whole different take on the matter. Had a funny feeling about this fella from the off, and so, on the quiet, she gives us a key to his room: 101. We don't waste no time shimmying off, up the fire escape, into the first-floor corridor.

When we opened the door, well the sight that met us. It was nothing no girl should have to endure. The Victor guy was trying to bind Bertha with ropes and there sure weren't no consent there. This time I thought it right to produce my piece, so I got it out and told him to untie the lady.

Course, there was lots of explanations concerning the whys and the wherefores of what he was up to. None of it goes down well. Princeton Charming says to bind the crazy guy with his own ropes, while the rest of us go call the cops.

We left Sindy at reception on the phone, though, gotta say I wasn't too convinced the police would take it serious. They don't tend to, I've found.

As our part was played and now sorted, Bashful and I decide it's best to scatter. I don't want no uncomfortable questions about the gun and we like our privacy out there in the woods. Though it took some effort to get Whitey back in the car – she only wanted to invite Princeton back for supper!

There was no way we could have that.

Not with some of the girls on the run from their pasts.

And so, it was then that I concluded – Whitey was getting us too much unwanted attention and tying us into some far-out scrapes.

Things clearly weren't working out.

Back at the ranch I said my bit and we agreed it was getting out of hand. We really oughta sort the sow.

Yeah, Whitey needed some care, but we weren't the right fit for her.

Grumpy decides we should do some investigating into Whitey's story. Old Grumps had worked in some kind of capacity for law-and-order agencies and while we never knew what exactly, we did know she was smart, level and shrewd. So we let her follow her nose and put Whitey onto seamstress duties. Told her to make herself a pretty outfit. This, at last, seemed to absorb her and she began designing a long blue and yellow frock.

Took Grumpy just a few days to find Whitey's real name. Margarita Hunter.

After that it didn't take no time at all to sniff the family out.

Myself and Sneezy were nominated to visit, while the others took care of the farm and mines.

We hit the road and drove for a few hours before we came upon the small town of Castle. A few enquiries were made and we soon located Whitey's family house.

Now what do you think happened when we knocked?

I was bracing myself for a strumpet to come out all guns blazing, but the door was opened by a little lady, most homely, with salt-and-pepper hair in a bun. Demanding an audience with the father, I was led into the parlour. Mr Hunter and a younger girl were listening to the wireless. Sneezy stayed on the porch, just in case there was trouble. Or cut flowers.

So I asks the olds about Whitey, and the tale that came out, well at first I couldn't take it in. See there weren't ever *any* to-do with a stepmom. Mr and Mrs Hunter had been together for twenty-five years and were happily married with two children – Whitey and her sister Laura.

It was Whitey who turned her own self out.

According to Mrs Hunter, she could never really place herself as an ordinary gal from a regular family and used to insist she'd been adopted at birth. Her mama said sometimes she wished she was. Mrs Hunter admitted that Whitey's notion of her own special destiny had the rest of them a bit put out. But they held their tongues. Then one day, Whitey went to market and she didn't ever come back.

So we told them where she was.

Both mother and papa were sincerely relieved and rejoiced to hear that their Margarita was well and good. True she surely annoyed the heck out of them, but she was flesh and blood, wasn't she? And they missed her.

It was agreed that Mrs Hunter should pay us a visit and try to coax Whitey back. Then, with tears of joy in their eyes, the family embraced us and waved goodbye. They were decent people.

A few days later when back in the woods, we hears a knock at the door. And look who it is – only Whitey's mama! Sleepy answered and bade her come settle on a swing chair outside. When I came out the sun was still hanging over the hills and a peachy light was filling up our porch. Bashful ran off to fetch Whitey and Mrs Hunter made herself comfortable. Being such a lovely dear she had only turned up with a basket of fruit for us which she set on the floor.

Happy and Sneezy had heard our guest's arrival and wandered out to meet the lady too. Grumps came in from the mines around the same time so all of them got introduced to Mrs Hunter.

Sneezy is thanking her very kindly for the fruit, when Whitey comes down from her room and only stops dead and stares and stares when she sees who's on the porch. And well – oh my – the *hysterics*.

'She's a witch! She's a witch!' Whitey spat as she points her bony finger at her mom.

Not very pleasant for the poor old dear who's come all this way to see her daughter. So I gets up and I says to our girl, 'Look Whitey, this is your mama. She ain't no witch, she just a nice little lady come to see how you are. They want you back in Castle now and we, for our parts, well we do think it's best.'

'No, no, NO!' Whitey goes. 'She's disguised herself, that's what she's done. You see her as a harmless old lady, perhaps dull. But she's cast a glamour over you. Under that enchantment lies a heart as cold as ice.'

At this point Grumpy, who's not partial to ill manners, says 'Now Whitey, you hold your tongue. If you know what's good for you, you'll come over and we can all have a nice cup of joe.'

Whitey never liked to cross Grumps or Sneezy, and both of them had their mouths pinched into short straight lines. She got the message and upped onto the porch and takes a seat.

The rest of us passes round the fruit to give us something to do and make her mother feel better. Though Whitey was still playing up, acting disinclined to take the basket when it came her way. We all frowned at her hard. She went into a sulk until Sleepy says, 'If this is the way you treat your guests, then Margarita, you ain't having no supper party here. 'And so eventually Whitey takes an apple. You would have thought it might calm down but no sooner had Whitey bitten into it than she jumps to her feet, holds her throat and screams 'I am poisoned! Look what she done to me.' And promptly the girl falls to the floor.

Oh lordy.

To say we was gobsmacked is an understatement indeed: our jaws was hanging about round our knees.

But Mrs Hunter's as cool as a cucumber and she goes, 'Oh don't start that again, dear.'

As you can imagine we were all looking at Mrs Hunter with expectation, so the old dear adds, 'Oh, she started doing this when she was seven. She'll stay like that till someone wakens her with a kiss. We used to get her cousin Henry over till he got the braces put on, then that wouldn't work no more. You'll need to find a man she likes to do the duty or she'll be like that till Christmas.'

Then she gets to her feet, 'I tried …' picks up the empty basket and heads for her car. 'Thank you for the beverage. Let us know how it goes.' And then, just like that, she's gone.

Leaving us with a comatose Whitey.

Grumpy was up for just letting her alone and announced she was going to the movies, just to see what happened next. But Sneezy and Bashful were more concerned.

Dopey fetched my bag so I got out my scope and had a listen to her heart. Turned out she had one, which was a surprise considering the way she

treated her kin. So I told the others she was just fine
– play-acting.

As night was falling, Bashful says, 'Let's just put
her up on the table so she's out of the way of the
chipmunks. They like a nip, don't theys?'

We took up each arm and each leg, Sleepy took
her head, then we swung her up onto the glass-
topped table. She didn't move, just snorted a bit,
like she liked it. Sneezy put out the flowers that
Grumpy had brought home and Happy arranged
them around her so she looks like a real sleeping
princess, and remarks on it, like it might rouse her.

But – nothing.

Back inside we called a house meeting.

'So who we gonna get to wake her?' asks Dopey.
And we all scratched our heads.

Then I pipe up, 'Kind of obvious, ain't it? We've got
to get in touch with that agent – Princeton Charming.'

And Grumpy murmurs thoughtfully, 'Hmmm.
I'm wondering if she planned this all along.'

But no one's got any better ideas.

So next day off Bashful goes back to the strip on
the hunt for Princeton Charming.

We all cross our fingers and toes and get back
to work with Whitey out there on the porch
pretend-snoring.

Later that afternoon up turns Bashful with Princeton Charming in tow, I was pleased to see. And he had some news for us about Victor the Palaeontologist, but it was heavy.

'He did wrong to that girl but still the authorities let him off with a caution,' he told us. 'Though in my books, this punishment sure don't fit the crime.'

'Yeah well, that's life,' concluded Grumpy. 'Lady Justice ain't able to do right to her own her kind. Not when her judgement is applied by those men.'

We thought about it, and then Happy went, 'Ain't that a true thing.'

'Same reason why yous all ended up here,' I confirmed.

And we could have gone on a bit longer, perhaps cooked up a plan of our own, but we was interrupted by a loud snore from the table.

'Ah, Whitey,' says Dopey. 'We had almost forgot.'

'You gotta kiss her,' Sneezy told Princeton.

He'd already been briefed by Bashful so it didn't take him no time at all to take to the task. Bending over Whitey, he puckered up and moved down straight to her mouth, planting his lips right on hers, giving her a long, hard and loud smacker.

I'm a cynic, myself, but it was kinda romantic.

Looked like he was starting to enjoy it too which meant it was time for us all to cough him out of it.

Heeding our snuffles, the agent pulled himself back, though he was regarding Whitey with a dazed look on his face.

We could all see something had passed between them.

Whitey, for her part, opened her eyes right up. 'Oh my Princeton!' says she. 'You have awakened me.' And she kisses him again and starts to tell him all about her stepmom, the witch and the poisoned apple.

When she's finished, he strokes his chin.

I couldn't read the expression on his face.

So I said to him, 'She's made it all up.'

But he shakes his head and says, 'Don't care. It's a good story.'

Then Happy comes in with, 'No one would believe that if you put it on screen.'

Princeton, however, pauses, all thoughtful for a moment. Then he says, 'I've got a contact in animation.' And bends back over Whitey. 'You should meet my friend, Walt.'

And the rest of the pantomime, as they say, is history.

(Oh no it isn't.)

(Oh yes it is.)

THIRTEEN

The day was scorching and although they had just finished breakfast Finn was already sweating in the sunshine. Fiona and Callum were in good spirits, jostling to get onto the air-conditioned coach, and laughing at the foreign family who, they had all observed, insisted on being first at the hotel buffet and claiming the best sunbeds around the pool with numerous towels, inflatables and robes. Somehow Fiona had wriggled her way almost to the front of the queue for the daytrip to Teras. The family had not taken this well, especially as their adolescent son, currently first in the line, was now stranded.

Fiona turned back to the mother, who was insisting in broken English that she should accompany her son.

'Sorry,' Fiona breezed with obvious insincerity. 'Don't understand. Can't *sprechen sie Deutsch*.'

Callum nudged her and tutted. 'Behave!' he grinned.

Finn might have attempted to mollify Fiona and tried to assist with the mother's conquest of the numero uno position alongside her son, were it not for the boy's countenance. He looked rather more peaceful than he had all week. Finn had noticed how the boy seemed to detach himself from the rest of the family at mealtimes. On their first night at the hotel the three friends hadn't been quite sure of how the evening meals were going to work. There was a brochure in the room, but no one could be bothered to read it so they had wandered down to the restaurant and sat around smoking and drinking while a small crowd of hungry diners gathered outside the closed doors. The family, the ladies in crop tops and shorts, gents in sandals and budgie smugglers, had shown up and then marched to the front where they leant against the doors, blocking access for everyone else.

When the waiter opened up, the same family stampeded to the buffet, eager to get first dibs on the starters. Finn noted the boy trailed wearily behind them. The rest of his group had not seemed to notice him joining their table fifteen minutes later with a modest selection of food on his plate and a glass of water. While the adults, two couples – possibly a brother and sister and their spouses (Finn hadn't worked it out yet) – got straight down to the business of imbibing as much free wine as they could, the boy produced a slim German novel and read it silently, barely attracting anything more than a nod from his parents.

Even the other children ignored him. There were two older teenage boys, who seemed to get on with each other well, if boisterously. One had fair sandy hair, a turned-up freckly nose viciously sunburnt. He seemed to belong to the blonde woman and her ginger husband. The other teen already sported a thick black moustache. He was plump, like the older mother with frizzy hair. This woman was with the copper-haired man wearing thick glasses. Finn could tell, as they had matching tattoos – some football team he'd never heard of. The man was tall and gangly. The thirteen-year-old seemed to take after him – in physique. But where the child was quiet, the father was loud with a shrill, grating laugh. Finn hadn't heard the boy laugh yet. Not at all. The other kids exuded the perky energy of their parents, which awkwardly highlighted the boy's languor. The youngest family member was a primary-school-age chubby girl with pink cheeks and a square face who had made friends with another little girl on a different table and went and sat there and giggled at mealtimes. Apart from Tuesday. Tuesday had been the boy's birthday. Finn and his friends had just entered the restaurant as a waiter was carrying a large cake over to the family's table. Sparklers blazed away on blue icing with a large flaming number '13'. Finn had caught the kid's eye as the waiter set the confectionary in front of him. The rest of his extended family were clapping and chanting 'Happy Birthday to you', encouraging, or possibly scaring, other tables into joining in. The boy was mortified.

Finn, Fiona and Callum had waited at the sides, showing some decorum, while the song finished.

The boy winced and blew out his '13'.

'Thirteen,' Finn commented. 'A painful age.'

'Better be careful,' Fiona retorted glibly.

'What do you mean?' Callum nuzzled her exposed neck and nipped it with his lips.

'Thirteen,' she said. 'Unlucky for some, innit.'

'You're nuts,' said Callum and kissed her.

Oh god, thought Finn, they're off. He would have to stay out for a while after dinner tonight.

The family room had been a good idea in principle when he decided to holiday with his friends. It meant they could split the cost three ways and keep expenditure down. A room of his own was completely unaffordable. Sharing like this would have been his only opportunity to see the Maldives at Christmas. Of course, nobody could have foreseen the consequent lockdown that scrapped all such plans. They had argued with the travel agents and managed to get something in the Mediterranean at this later date. But for the same price, irritatingly. Nor had Finn anticipated the aphrodisiac qualities of sunshine and the unexpected awkwardness of cohabiting with a couple for a week.

The three had come to an unspoken agreement that he would stay out of the room after dinner and go and drink by the pool in order that Fiona and Callum could have some 'quality time'. And yes, that was a euphemism.

A couple of days in a row, the quality time had gone on for a good few hours. Last night the couple had not joined him at the bar till 1 a.m. Not that it really mattered. Finn had spied the boy down there, lounging on a sunbed with white chiffon curtains and reading a novel. After a while he noticed he had gone, leaving his book there, face down and splayed.

Intrigued, Finn sauntered over and casually glanced at it. In the dim evening light, he saw that the cover featured an oil painting of a young man with a disaffected air, reclining on a sofa. The author's name hinted at German ancestry, he thought: Husymans. Its title *Gegen den Strich*. A quick google suggested the book was altogether too mature for a thirteen-year-old. He had no time to pursue the matter further, though. The boy appeared at the end of the bar, returning to his lounger, followed in by Fiona and Callum.

Finn came away with a distinct feeling he had intruded on something private, and hastened back to his table where he waved Fiona and Callum over, pretending he had been there all the time. They ordered drinks and began chatting idly about the heat of the night. Finn looked back at the chiffon-draped recliner. The mum, dad, aunt and uncle were calling the boy to bed. The four adults, in vests with damp patches, tight shorts and flip flops, were visibly inebriated. Their voices, even louder than usual, drew disapproving glances from those gathered round the bar. The boy began to disentangle himself from the bed, but not quickly enough for the uncle who said something he clearly thought hilarious. Getting no response from the child, he plucked the novel from his hands. Dangling it before the boy's eyes like a carrot, he grinned and laughed in a dribbly, wild manner. As the child reached for the book, in a moment of ill-judged spontaneity, his uncle chucked it over his shoulder.

Those in the bar unable to disengage from the unfolding incident watched on in dismay as the novel sailed up over the tiles and fell with a plop into the pool.

For a moment everything quietened, the only noise a tinny Eurotrashy dance track. In the water, the book's pages spread out like a fan. It seemed to Finn that the whole place, right then, was holding its breath, waiting to see what might happen next. Then the boy's father broke the spell and burst out laughing. The rest of the family joined him. All except the boy, who pelted over to the water's edge. Finn watched with a wrinkled forehead as he knelt down and tried to save the slowly sinking pages. The dad went over and pretended to aim a kick at his rear. The mother pulled him away and shook her head, but she was still laughing.

'Bunch of planks,' Finn muttered under his breath.

Callum heard him. 'Poor kid,' he said.

'She's getting it now,' Fiona commented. A bartender had come over with a hook for the blinds and was helping to fish the book out. 'Imagine having parents like that.'

'Yeah,' said Finn. Although his had not been cruel, he had never felt great kinship with his mum and dad. Where he liked books and music, they liked sport and shopping. He liked to travel – they preferred new cars and carpets. He still loved them and they him.

But he could see here this family dynamic was very different.

The barmaid handed the soggy mess to the boy. His face, Finn noted, was not crumpled or caved in as he had expected, but firm, resigned, stoic. The boy thanked her politely then followed his family into the hotel, leaving behind him a trail of sad little drips.

'Too much wine, they have,' said their waiter, laying down the beers on the table and nodding after the boy's parents. 'Too much.'

The mood had changed. All three of the friends felt it, so drank the lagers quickly then retired. They needed to be up fairly early for the trip anyway.

This morning though, Finn was tired and heavy and dehydrated, and relieved enormously when the driver opened the coach doors and invited them in.

When he got onto the vehicle, he saw that Fiona and Callum had laid claim to the front seats behind the driver. The boy was on the seats the other side of the aisle, sitting near the window. Fiona had put her bag on the seat next to him.

'Go on, Finn,' she hissed, 'Before the "Frau hairy mama" gets in.'

Finn cringed. He was sure the boy spoke English. 'Do you mind if I sit here?' he asked him.

The boy turned his eyes on Finn. They were huge and dark and shiny. Finn thought he saw recognition flare, but the boy simply shrugged his scrawny shoulders.

'It's not up to him, is it?' Fiona piped up. 'Free country.'

At that point the German family pushed past and took the seats behind them. The mother pushed a bottle of juice between the headrests, knocking Finn's cap off. She didn't apologise, but the boy had seen and looked at Finn, his cheeks beginning to flush.

'I apologise,' he said in a small voice, when the hand had withdrawn.

'It's okay,' Finn answered. 'You can choose your friends but you can't choose your family,' he said, as Fiona threw a can of beer onto his lap. Maybe he should have done that more thoughtfully too.

'It's only ten o'clock,' Finn replied and threw it back.

'We're on holiday,' said Callum and caught it. 'Waste not want not.' And he pulled back the ring cap.

Finn turned to the boy, who had been watching, and shrugged. A thin wisp of something that very nearly became a smile touched his lips.

'I'm Finn,' he introduced himself.

The boy nodded, 'Karl,' then dropped his eyes and began to rummage through his rucksack, finally fishing out a thin guidebook.

Finn took this as a hint and closed his eyes. The engine started and, at last, the air-conditioning kicked in.

When he next looked up, they were out on the coastal road. The Mediterranean Sea spread out beneath the cliffs, sparkling like an azure, jewel-encrusted cloak.

The boy was reading the guide.

'Anything in there about the island?' Finn asked.

The boy, Karl, looked up, an expression of startled indignance on his face, as if he had forgotten he was sharing his space with another human being. He grimaced with vague disapproval but said, 'Teras. Yes.'

Finn waited for a while as Karl flicked back a few pages.

'Teras means wonders or gifts. The island of Teras,' Karl translated as he read, 'has a patched, chequered, history.'

As he suspected, the boy's English was excellent. Finn watched his eyes narrow and his brow contract as he concentrated. He was good, though he stumbled over a word in his narration and held the book up to Finn and pointed at it.

'Ah,' said Finn in what he thought was a kindly paternal tone. 'Byzantium. That's a hard word.'

Karl repeated it several times in accented English, until he had got the hang of it. Finn's eyes strayed across the page he was holding. There was a doodle in the margin in biro: a self-portrait he thought.

'Is that you?' he asked Karl, pointing to a neat side parting, drawn above sad, almond-shaped eyes, a very slender neck and upturned nose.

'Oh, yes,' the boy replied.

'Very good,' said Finn, wondering why Karl had drawn on a frown rather than a smile as other children his age did.

The boy merely shrugged and continued on. 'And it fell into dis …' Karl struggled. 'What is when the buildings are not maintained? They crumble.'

'Disrepair?' offered Finn.

'Yes!' A flicker of triumph passed over Karl's face. 'Disrepair. The island became a small fishing community. Until ...' he glanced up at Finn, and paused to lick his lips. 'Until the nineteen century.'

'Nineteenth,' Finn suggested, but this time Karl did not take his recommendation on board. He seemed eager to head on into what was interesting him.

'When Teras succumbed to the disease of ...' again he paused. 'Die Lepra.' He looked up at Finn. 'Sores, infection, grotesque.'

Finn looked at the word. 'Leprosy?'

Karl nodded silently. 'The monastery beside the church of Mary became an orphanage for children of the infected. Thought to be contagious themselves, most were kept there for the rest of their lives with little contact to ... wait!' He corrected himself. 'Little contact *with* the outside world.'

He checked Finn's face for a reaction then said, 'They had no mirrors. Because the lepers – they did not want to see their own faces.'

'Oh,' Finn shuddered. 'How awful. Poor children. And to think of them locked up there, away from everyone.'

Karl looked into his eyes. 'It's not so bad, I think,' he said.

Surprised by this confession, Finn gasped. 'You don't mean that,' he began, but a hand came through the headrests and caught his cheek.

'Excuse me,' said a voice overhead.

Finn looked up and was almost engulfed by a pair of pendulous breasts, hanging over him. Barely covered by a tight lycra dress, Karl's mother clearly had no concept of other people's personal space. Or maybe she didn't care. Finn caught a whiff of body odour and last night's wine.

'Karl!' his mother barked. 'Sei bereit, wir sind fast da.' Then she withdrew.

Finn straightened up once more. He wasn't sure what had been said, but Karl's shoulders now sagged. He closed the guidebook and stowed it away in his knapsack.

Up ahead he realised that they were winding down a road into a little harbour. Small boats bobbed up and down in the waves. Shops and bars clustered around the quay.

'Pretty!' cooed Fiona across the aisle. 'Look Finn. There's the boat.' She pointed to a wooden vessel of about thirty feet with glass windows and seating up on the deck.

Karl's mother appeared in the aisle, reached across Finn. She took hold of Karl's arm and pulled the boy up and over. It was quite a rough manoeuvre, but Karl barely batted an eyelid. Instead, he let his mother stand him in front of her and push his shoulders so that he faced the front of the bus. The rest of his family lined up behind them.

'Er, we're at the front actually,' he heard Fiona mutter. She was roundly ignored.

'Oh, it's all right, Fi,' Finn called over them. 'We've all got to get on the boat.'

Karl sent him a slow resigned sigh and rolled his eyes.

In the event, there was no need whatsoever to have rushed. The bus had not been packed and there was space on the ferry to seat everyone comfortably with their friends or families. The three pals had managed to get a little space out on the prow and sat on a section of raised deck as the boat made its way over the water. A wind came up and ruffled their hair.

The island rose out of the sea. Full of rust-coloured boulders and arid shrubs, punctured with holes and cavities, you could make out the signs of an old fortification to the west.

Despite the glorious sunshine and cloudless sky Finn felt a balloon of depression float up from his stomach. What would it have been like, he wondered, to be imprisoned here on this floating rock? He didn't want to think about it, so took a beer from Callum's pack.

Soon they had drawn up alongside a jetty. Two by two they disembarked, walking down a narrow wooden gangplank, and went ashore. Fiona and Callum were anxious that the three of them 'do their own thing' and quickly separated from the tourist throng who had already started moving along the main road in herd formation to the ruins at the top.

Instead, the friends stopped at a small café and had lunch, then decided to go east around the island, looking for a bay that had been recommended to Callum by a drunk Scotsman the day before.

'It's beautiful, apparently,' said Callum. 'Hardly anyone there.'

'Great,' said Fiona. She was flushed from the beer and clapped her hands. 'We can go skinny dipping.'

Finn wasn't so keen on that, but he could do with a swim. The heat was becoming oppressive, and he realised he had left his cap on the coach.

After forty-five minutes they reached the bay. There were a handful of other people on the beach, which meant that, thankfully, Fiona had to keep her clothes on. The water though was delicious. Almost warm.

'It's like a bath!' Fiona screamed as they ran into the waves.

'Want your back scrubbed?' asked Callum.

When he had cooled down Finn made an excuse about wanting to see the ruins while they still had time. The increasingly amorous couple weren't interested, which was a relief, so he dried himself and set off up the hill. Although he'd only used it as an excuse, he was surprised to find that, since his conversation with Karl, he appeared to have already resolved to see the church and monastery. Or the orphanage, as it had become. Then a prison.

He knew that the village on Teras had been abandoned after the war, and was vaguely aware of a salacious scandal. That much had been alluded to on the leaflet advertising the trip. He hadn't taken too much notice of it at the time, grateful only to get out of the claustrophobic resort. But thinking back now he had the impression of a cover-up. Ironically, however, the mystery and enigma surrounding the island had grown, its tainted reputation only attracted yet more tourists.

He continued upwards. The slope was steeper than he realised, and Finn had to rest several times before he finally reached the summit. He was slower physically than he had imagined he would be. His limbs were ageing, despite the fact he still thought of himself as a young man.

Though the view was worth the effort.

He stood at the top, panting, and looked east across to the little harbour from which they had come. The bay with its houses and shops and boats glittered like a diamond bracelet in the afternoon sun. Beyond it a bank of dark clouds, which suggested cooler climes, was rolling their way. How strange, he thought, that there is a storm coming on such a day. The sky due south that had been a perfect cornflower blue out of the coach window this morning was now taking on lilac-grey colouring. Above him, however, the sun continued to glare down, bald and blind, drying out even further the ever-parched air and tensing the rocky landscape.

On his back and neck, exposed skin not protected by his vest was burning. He could feel the heat coming off his body and cursed himself for not applying sunscreen in the morning. Fiona usually had some but he'd been in such a hurry to leave the cove that he hadn't thought about asking. Never mind. There was only a couple of hours left. He'd better get a move on.

Ahead, across a dusty plain that may have once been a piazza or square, stood a low stone wall. The air above it shimmered. Approaching, he saw it was the border of a cemetery containing a number of flat stone graves.

He climbed over.

Many of the slabs were unmarked, weather-beaten and smooth, but there were some whose inscriptions had not yet been obliterated by the elements. He tried to translate those. The people here were old, most buried hundreds of years ago. Again, he felt chronically aware of his age, and wondered how many years he would have ahead of him. Had he lived half of his life already? No, he shook his head. Intimations of mortality should not come to you on holiday. It was wrong. He was picking up on a residual overlay of emotion that previous visitors to the graves had left behind. Nevertheless, he found the monuments intriguing and would have liked to have spent longer here, but there was little shadow and time was running out.

As he made his way across the cemetery, he noted a square section of tombs in the corner by the church. A smaller size. Finn eyed the engravings. The names were hard to make out but he could see from the birthdates and death dates most were children. A cluster of them appeared to have died together at the end of 1882. Why would that be? Leprosy? Did it do that? Go on killing sprees? Or could it have been something else? *Someone* else eager to eradicate the risk of infection? Wow, Finn thought to himself, that was morbid. Where had that notion come from? It was not like him to harbour such darkness. Must be the cemetery kindling with the haunting history Karl had relayed.

Eager to shake off the queer feeling, he straightened up and made his way towards the exit, wind brushing against his face. It was bolder now, daring to blow out his hair. The storm was getting closer, the air around him beginning to dim. Soon the sun would be covered and the light would scatter.

Finn glanced at his watch. Four o'clock. Lord, he had spent more time here than intended. He should be back on the boat in fifty minutes. The rest of the tourists would likely be returning to the harbour now for a quick drink before they clambered aboard the ferry. What would the captain think of the mean sky above him? Would he want to make a move early, before the storm rained down and tossed the harbour boats around like toys in the bath? Surely he'd not leave till all passengers were accounted for? Though the locals didn't seem as rigorous with their

Health and Safety procedures as the authorities back home.

'I'll be quick,' Finn said to no one but the crumbling dust of buried corpses.

A low rumble of thunder came up from the south-east.

He drank the last of his water and left the cemetery, coming out onto a narrow road. The church, catching the last of the sun's rays, glimmered at the end. It was hard to miss – the cross on its spire cast a long, deep shadow to the east. Finn walked into it, enjoying the brief drop in temperature, then orientated himself towards St Mary's. Or Santa María de los Dolores as was its correct name, apparently. Our Lady of Sorrows. Appropriate for this island with its history he thought, as he let himself in through the wooden door.

The church was small, more of a chapel really. Whitewashed and spare, the only artefact that interested him was a statue of Mary with seven daggers thrust into her. The Madonna stared at him, accusation in her eyes. Or so he thought. Why would she do that? No, no, she wasn't doing anything. It was his mind genuflecting into lapsed obedience. He could never get away from the feeling that he was being watched whenever he was in church. But then you were meant to think like that weren't you? It was part of the creed. Christianity was a peculiar religion, he reflected.

As if disagreeing, the heavens suddenly broke with a sonorous crash. Rain started battering the vaulted roof.

Finn dashed to the door, as quick as his heat-stroked limbs could carry him, and looked out. At first he was confused by the strangeness of the scene, but then he realised this was not the door through which he had come, but a side entrance that led onto a narrow square. It was not night, he knew, but the sun had gone, obscured by dark, angry clouds that seemed so low he thought for a moment he might reach up and touch them.

Opposite the church stood a long, flat building, its monotonous contour broken only by a solitary bell tower. The metallic sign over a heavy stone doorway indicated that this was the orphanage. Rain was coming down, gathering in puddles on the ground and it was there, by a quickly forming pool, a few metres away, that Finn spotted the boy, Karl. Why was he on his own? Finn darted a look, left and right and around the square for the rest of his family, but it was empty.

He called out his name. Karl however appeared hypnotised: something was sucking in his attention.

The young lad was paying little heed to the whirling downpour.

Surely the boy was too exposed there, Finn worried? Out in the open, standing in a courtyard at the top of a hill, the highest ground for miles?

'Karl!' Finn called again but the wind whipped his words away.

Above the island the sky roared.

Finn couldn't let him stand there on his own, exposed to lightning. He rushed into the elements.

Once more thunder exploded like a canon ricocheting across the bay, echoing off the walls around them, vibrating through the ground.

Finn paused, overwhelmed by sensory onslaught. He breathed in deeply.

The air was animated, energised by electricity. It made him feel weird, super-alive, hypersensitive, aware of the violence in the sky and land, aware of this little patch of the world, of life existing at particle level, as it had done from the beginning of time when the earth was forming out of spraying lava, to its future burning to a cinder under the relentless sun.

He shook his head, exhaled, and the feeling came out of him. With intense effort he moved himself, putting one foot after another till he reached the boy.

Karl's hair and clothes were sodden. He remained unaware of Finn, his eyes locked, trancelike.

Reaching out, Finn touched his arm. 'Karl! We have to get to shelter. It's dangerous here. The storm …'

The boy reluctantly let go of his gaze and shifted his eyes from the wall to Finn's face.

'You have come,' his voice faltered, rusty, as if it hadn't been used for years. 'Can you feel it?'

Finn's fingers tightened on the boy's skinny arm. 'Not now,' he began to shake him, 'we should get inside.'

But still Karl did not move. 'The children,' he said. 'They have drawed themselves in.'

An instinct within Finn warned him he should not look, but Karl's compulsion was too fascinating, too strong, for him to resist.

'The mural,' the boy called above the wind and rain.

And he turned and saw it.

This was what had captured Karl so.

Painted onto the wall, Finn's brain initially perceived it as a religious cartoon or pastiche, low and narrow and reaching across the whole length of the wall.

Then, with a shock, he realised what it was – exactly.

They had daubed their own images onto the wall so that they resembled a long unearthly choir, a host of strange beings. The front row had been drawn by young children. These were not the self-portraits of leprosy sufferers, but idealised versions of themselves, such as all children draw: round faces, curly hair, stick arms and legs. Five of them were pictured sitting behind a table, impressionistic and sweet, primitive in their execution – and yet, to the eye, full of a particular energy, as if they had painted their better selves, their souls, into the picture.

Lightning struck something wooden nearby. The flash lit up the wall and – for a moment – he saw the children blink.

No.

It couldn't be.

He moved up over the uppermost portraits and saw that they were different. More accomplished, sketched by older children aware of their own deformities and difference, misshapen and odd, but still carved with strange, luminous smiles. There were seven there, shining in the darkness.

The sight of them made Finn instantly sad, yet exhilarated, as if he was being shown something tragic and holy, and exclusive. Twelve dead children sitting down to a feast. Even their pose was sacred, he thought, reminiscent of Da Vinci's *Last Supper*.

An impulse was growing inside, urging him to step closer to the paintings, to see them more clearly, to allow himself to be pulled into them. Yet, another part of his being warned him to wait, to get the boy to shelter.

He breathed in and found his nostrils fill with the scent of danger. He was about to back away with the intention of scooping Karl into his arms and carrying him into the church, when, all at once, the air blazed with a searing atomic-white flash. A sudden shower of sparks rained down as the bell clanged and exploded above them. He glanced up in time to see a single streak of lightning discharge and fork, crackling, down through the wall, dazzling him, but also simultaneously illuminating everything, *everything*. For, to this day he insists that, though it was over in a fraction of a second, right then time slowed to a point.

And, in that frozen instant, out of the corner of his eyes he saw the children again blink and smile. Slowly. Neurones at the base of his neck, somewhere in the primal part of his brain, flared, and he understood that these were not primitive wall paintings but actual living beings. Sealed in. Safe.

It was, he would attest in future years, as if he glimpsed behind the surface of the wall, as if he had gone through the television screen, into the place where all mysteries are solved.

The space there was sunny, green, sweet, full of children's playground sounds, laughter and songs, and sugary smells. It was, he would go on to describe, like seeing what the portraits did when they relaxed, when no one else was around, watching how statues moved after the galleries closed, and learning what the trees said when there was no one to hear them fall. An invitation into a spectral world, a moment of afterlife, another's dream.

It was just an instant, but that was what his brain absorbed.

Then time caught up with itself again and Finn's body moved. Fast. His head continued to turn away, his vision settling on Karl. The boy's arms were up in the air, his entire form encased in the light of hundreds of millions of volts.

The child was hurled onto the ground, his eyes closed, arms thrown outwards.

Thunder came down over them. Loud like hammers on metal.

Finn raced to Karl. Kneeling down he moved his ear to the boy's chest. The child's vest top was singed round the neck and smelled of smoke, but he was breathing.

Think, think! Finn ordered himself silently. What to do?

He tapped Karl's cheek, but the boy was out cold, rain falling on his long dark eyelashes. 'Wake up!' Finn shouted.

To his astonishment the boy's eyes snapped open.

And looked into him.

The gaze, Finn thought, the intensity …

He understood immediately that something had changed.

Deep brown and dark, physically similar to Karl's, these eyes were possessed by a very different energy, a fresh and bright wildness. The boy bolted upright and looked around, shaking the raindrops from his hair. Despite the immense physical and electrical shock he had just been through, the child broke into a laugh.

'Soy libre!' The boy who was Karl, scrambled to his feet. 'Soy libre! Free!'

His hands touched the air with joy and he laughed once more. Mouth half open in awe, he looked around hastily, face lit up with excitement, the unexpected brilliance of possibilities. 'Estarán en el embarcadero. Esperandome ...' and with that he broke into a run, springing through the archway, out onto the main track that led down to the harbour.

Finn, who was still kneeling where Karl had fallen, looked after him, stunned and bewildered by what he had witnessed, or thought he had witnessed. As he hauled himself to a standing position, his mind reeled. Strange, unknown thoughts circled him.

A horn went off somewhere down on the quay. It startled him. The ferry! He must hurry, he would think about this later.

Finn shuffled across the courtyard, his limbs moving in a slow cumbersome manner as if they belonged to someone else.

As he reached the end of the orphanage, just before exiting the courtyard, he took one last glance at the mural. It was lifeless now, a flat, two-dimensional rendering, a commemoration of the children of Teras drawn in their own hand.

Though, what was that?

One singular portrait caught his eye. It was set back from the top row and higher than those surrounding it. He was sure it had not been there before.

Finn took a heavy step towards it then hesitated. He did not want to miss the boat and be left on the island. But there was something about this fresh painting that would not let him go without a final look.

He inched closer and gasped.

There it was – a portrait of Karl, sketched just as he had seen it in the margins of his guidebook. The image had the same side parting of unkempt moppy hair, a thin neck and button nose. But the eyes, the eyes were bright. Above his head, at the top of the tableau, he saw, a star had appeared. Five-pointed and shining vividly, extraordinarily, from the mural.

Finn reached out and touched the face. It was hot, the paint sizzling as it dried.

He flinched and stepped back, uncomprehending.

As the ferry blew its final horn, he realised.

At last.

The boy was finally smiling.

STRING OF LIGHTS

Rozalie sits alone by the window. She turns the ring on her gnarled finger, a promise never fulfilled. The night darkens slowly. Lights twinkling in the windows of cottages across the fields send sweet clouds of memory to her.

She remembers a time before the Great War. Her mother, at the looking glass, combing out flaxen hair. Candles in glass holders spread across the surface, like Christmas. Darkness outside pressing hard against frost-rimed windows. The room timbered like a ship's cabin, as warm as a womb. Rozalie, just a child, sitting on her parents' bed piled high with pillows and covered in silk sails, watching.

Privileged.

Allowed this glimpse, though she knew not why.

Her mother was in good spirits that night, slightly in love with her reflection. She hummed a gay tune as she brushed. Surrounded by burnished lamps, caught between the round globes of their auras, Emma's hair shone and glimmered. And Rozalie remembers how she had thought at that very moment her mother to be the most beautiful woman alive. Quite like an angel. A fairy from the top of a fir tree. A creature not of this earth. She recalls the soft glow of her mother's cheeks, her skin the colour of fine cream and how, when Emma's lips opened like a rosebud in early May, the air about her sighed in adoration.

And her mother laughed, a tinkle like a bell in a stream, and said, 'Did I ever tell you about the Archduke, my child? Did I ever talk of that night?'

Rozalie knew the story, of course, but she said, 'No Mama.'

And Emma said, 'Well then, my dear, you are in for a treat.'

So Rozalie plumped the pillows under her belly and sank onto them, hands cradling her chin, and she opened her rosebud mouth and drank her mother in.

'It was quite a night,' Emma trilled. 'I had been a guest of the Novaks that summer. And it had been particularly hot. We had spent most of the day in the park by the boating lake. I had been out in a pretty blue boat with Izak, their youngest, but when the sun burned brightest at noon we sailed to shore and drank iced tea in the shade of the poplars. Janička, my school friend, and the Novaks' eldest daughter, would not rest however. She was a funny thing – full of jest and defiance. Boyish, with a snub nose and always cutting her hair, which was presently short and patchy and made her look much younger than her years. Rather too quick with her tongue. Really, that was why I liked her so much. We had fun. But that day Janička was contrary for the sake of controversy. Even I was beginning to find her tiresome. When she announced it was her turn to go out on the lake none could stop her. She was as headstrong as an untrained mare. My father did not approve of the friendship. Not entirely. However, the Novaks had been bred impeccably and were extremely well connected, which helped him to overcome his objections to my trip. He was a terrible snob.

'Janička stayed out far too long. We called to her from under the trees to 'come in' but she would not. The boatman grew anxious and waved at her too. But still Janička did not return. Madam Novak announced it was time to leave – Janička began to sing and pretend she could not hear her. It was not until her father, growing weary and vexed, decided we should gather up our belongings and withdraw to the carriage without her that, unwilling to walk home alone, Janička finally bent the boat to the jetty.

'Her mother was most displeased. Janička had delayed our return to the villa. That night there was to be a special ball and there were many preparations to make. I was to sit with Izak and keep him company. Madam Novak chided Janička and said she had a mind to make her stay in with her brother instead. Surely prophetic words because, no sooner had we arrived back at the Novaks, than Janička took sick from the sun. The poor thing was most nauseous and had to be put to bed at once.

'Now someone surely was watching over me that night,' said her mother, turning away from the mirror and gifting Rosalie with the light in her face, 'for once they had seen to their daughter, the Novaks asked if I would like to come in her place!

'Oh,' said Emma. 'I could not believe it. Of course, I felt for Janička, but I had never been to a ball and could not conceal my delight. I accepted immediately.' She clapped her hands beneath her bosom, close to her heart. 'Madam Novak fetched me Janička's ballgown. You see, we were around the same size and oh, it was satin and the colour of pearls. In truth, it suited me more than Janička. My complexion caused it to shine. And a corsage, yes! A large, red rose and,' she said, remembering, 'violets. Just enough to bring out the colour of my eyes. The maid coiled my hair and pinned it. Madam Novak herself touched my lips and cheeks with rouge. I was sprayed with Parisienne perfume, glossed with Egyptian oil and pulled tight into Chinese silk.'

She returned, greedily, to the looking glass 'My reflection revealed someone I had not seen before, but, oh my dear Rozalie, a woman who had been waiting to emerge.' She smiled at her younger self in the mirror, admiring the bloom that once existed there.

'It was too late to change the announcement,' she continued, breathlessly. 'So it was decided that, just for one night, I should be Janička. I was happy to play my part of course. I could not wait to get into the carriage, though I cannot remember the journey to the ball, only arriving at the palace. Well, I had never been anywhere like it. Lofty ceilings with intricate plasterwork shaped into leaves and squirrels, and three magnificent crystal chandeliers that hung down over the most colourful and elegant crowd.'

Rozalie drank in her mother's luminescence. 'You know, darling, that when I was announced, at the top of the great staircase, all heads turned to look at me. Me! Can you imagine?'

Rozalie could. She had pictured it many, many times before.

'We descended the stairs slowly. It didn't take me long to see him there. Such a man: statuesque, built like a warrior, fetching for his age. Every single person in that ballroom was aware of his presence. He glided through the room in a cocoon, untouched by the dancing and excited chatters of those who sought his attention. The Archduke himself!

'The Novaks spotted some friends so we made our way to their corner. They were most amiable people. Now, I was talking to their daughter when it happened. I saw her eyes move over my shoulder for a moment, then she dropped them to the floor. Her cheeks began to redden. Madam Novak fluttered her fan quickly and smiled with purpose in my direction. I could feel eyes on my back and turned round.

'There he was, requesting to be introduced – to me! And that's how it started. He nodded with approval when I curtseyed. He was handsome, it was plain to see, and when he held out his hand to dance with me, I froze. Several heartbeats passed. I remember how the ballroom wheeled around and receded, so that, for a moment, we were locked into the light of each other's eyes as if we were the only two people in the world. Then Madam Novak nudged me and broke the spell. I took his arm and we made our way to the dancers and he said, "Don't be afraid, I will lead you." I didn't know what to say, so remained silent till, as we began a slow waltz, he whispered, "You bring to my mind the wings of butterflies."

'Butterflies! It was an intense, extraordinary moment. I think I blushed. All eyes were upon us as we sailed across the floor. He was light on his feet for such a man. The orchestra played and the night wore on and still he refused to relinquish me. I, however, was becoming thirsty. Eventually the Archduke stopped. There was sweat upon his brow – the night was hot and long and the exertion of the dance … He led me by my hand to a seat outside on the balcony where we sipped champagne.

"'It is absurd," he said. "Have I met you before?" Such strong features, such a noble brow. I was going to tell him "No, not at all", when Mr Novak appeared from nowhere and said, "There you are Janička!" You see, I had quite forgotten that I was meant to be someone else. And do you know what? The Archduke lifted my hand and kissed it. It felt natural. And he said, "I am enchanted, Janička."

'It was all so much that I suddenly felt light-headed and sparkly, completely unlike myself, and I laughed and laughed and the Archduke joined in too, and then Mr Novak, though he did not look like he meant it. For a moment, however, we were all caught in a glorious bubble of joy. But as we were catching our breath, a courtier appeared by the Archduke's side and beckoned him away on a matter of great importance. I could tell he did not want to leave, but affairs of state wait for no man. Mr Novak smiled as he excused himself. And off the Archduke went.

'His approval meant that dances followed, one after another. I was never without a partner. Madam Novak declared me the belle of the ball.

'We returned home late and sat in the drawing room tumbling our minds over the evening, laughing and gossiping. Oh what fun. It was only when I finally went to kiss the Novaks goodnight, they reminded me that I was to be Emma again. I would, they chuckled, have to explain to Janička how upon this sultry summer's night she had entranced the great Archduke.

'The next day we slept in. We were tired. The Novaks had given instructions to the staff not to disturb us. I awoke at a time that was not early but neither was it late, and descended to find Janička in the parlour most perplexed.

'When I asked what was troubling her, she replied that an Archduke had just paid a visit to see her. He had come with an apology for his premature withdrawal from the ball last night, which he did deliver apparently with evident speed and then immediately left!

'When I told Janička what had occurred we fell into fits of giggles. The Archduke had apologised for the dim lights in the ballroom and mumbled about underestimating her age, which he could see now was young in this present light.

A pause as her smile spread across her pink cheeks. 'And do you know what, Rozalie?'

She did, but said, 'No?'

Her mother hooted, loudly. 'He never went back to the Novaks again!' She looked into the mirror at her younger self. 'I often wonder if I had received him myself, not Janička …'

For a moment the child saw in her mother's face … someone else… another person … who had lived before her. And a sense of disconnection speared her being, as if a psychic umbilical cord had just been cut.

'But then you met father,' Rozalie prompted.

'Yes, yes, of course and he, oh he, was, *is*, my one true love.'

The little girl smiled, satisfied, willing a deafness to her mother's whispered 'And yet …'

And again, the cord tore.

'Love,' her mother said suddenly and with emphasis. Detecting a change in her daughter she got to her feet. 'Now let me brush your hair.'

And Rozalie let herself be pulled to her and seated in front of the gleaming mirror, all shining, thinking of what might be to come, of her own unborn merry pleasures and the possibility of love. And she breathed in the smell of Emma, her cream, and her lightness, watched her and felt the brush on her hair.

Her mother happy, girlish, flushed.

There, in that old world.

Before the Great War.

A world of light and of dreams.

Before the new world of suffering and guilt that took her own love away.

By the window Rozalie turns the ring on her finger, a promise made, doomed to die.

She cannot pull her mind from it.

ROGATIONTIDE

The blessing of the crops at Rogationtide was one of the most ancient ceremonies of the church. Thought to date from 468 AD in Gaul, it was delivered three days preceding Ascension Day. In the reign of Queen Elizabeth I orders were issued for the revival of this custom when the priest and parish would walk about the village and fields then return to the church to make their prayers. Curates were positioned out and about in the lanes to admonish those who did not follow the procession and make them join with the others to pray to God for an increase and abundance of the fruits of the earth.

The beautiful institution, however, had fallen into decay at the beginning of the twentieth century, although there had been a revival of some folk traditions in tandem with the rise in popularity of what was termed 'folk music'. Privately, Cissie dismissed the genre as another tangent of tawdry popular culture. It was vulgar and the rituals it limply resuscitated, such as the crowning of the May Queen or Flora Day, she derided as pale commercial fripperies embraced only by hippies, marijuana smokers, people who grew their hair long and did not wash their armpits. She was, however, fiercely proud of the fact that the Blessing of the Crops still took place annually on Northye Island. It had, in fact, never gone away, never been diluted, never softened nor been adapted to the whims and fashions of the age. The islanders had always kept their faith and observed the tradition, particular to this region, with unflinching dedication. Though some might see the invocations of the priest, who called ever upwards for divine intervention, as archaic, they knew this was fundamentally not so.

Which is why they prepared for it all year round.

Over the past couple of years, since the mid-seventies, there had been a few tourists who had attempted to infiltrate their ranks, intent on witnessing the ceremony. Of course they were well aware that it was a private and sacred ritual. Cissie, however, had observed that outsiders were often undisciplined when it came to curiosity. Because of this, in Northye, strangers were easily sniffed out. A couple of times the village men had discovered students in their midst, dressed like May Queens and Kings, pretending to be cousins or kin of one of the great Northye families. Such interlopers were dealt with swiftly and returned forthwith to the mainland, the threat of trespass and prosecution stinging their ears. And the boats of tourists eager to take part in this rite that was uniquely theirs had been dealt with so severely that all skippers in the vicinity made sure they were busy and booked with other activities come Rogationtide.

The rite belonged to Northye, as much as Northye belonged to the rite. The two were inextricably linked.

And jealously guarded.

Of course.

So the island had flourished and when a community prospers its folk do find their way to power. It was all about the money, Cissie knew. The money and the connections they fostered. For a small fee and the promise of good fortune Northye was now secured by a section of discreet officers who blocked off roads and patrolled the waters of the River Chelmer so that the islanders could enjoy their eccentric custom undisturbed. Or, as

Cissie expressed it, 'without violation'. And that was another gift from God that they should give praise for. Isolation was bliss, seclusion a comfort. In these days of television, telephones and radio, few people on the mainland kept themselves to themselves anymore. The world babbled continuously, trying to reach out and link people. With all the telephonic breakthroughs there was much talk of connection. Frightful. She could not imagine being absorbed by the greater world. The thought thoroughly unsettled her. But today was not a day to think of such horror. Today was the day Northye would count its blessings.

By the time she had got to the church the choir had already started the chant. Voices rang out over the heads of the swollen congregation, down the high street, across the cottages and over the fields. The land was flat here, fashioned acoustically by some dark creator so that the sounds of ritual might carry across his chosen domain.

Auxilium nostrum in nomine Domini.

Qui fecit cælum et terram

Dominus vobiscum

Et cum spiritu tuo.

Cissie knew it from beginning to end. It was part of the very fabric of her being. As she joined the chorus with lungs full and spirit brimming, the words thrummed in her blood and opened her up.

Down they went through the high street, past Williams the bakers, *Heel,* the shoe shop that Linda Smith opened a year ago, the Chantry family's convenience shop, and then *Hearts* the butchers – the most important of all.

The numbers gathered as they opened out into St Northye's field, the site made most holy by their namesake, who had, according to legend, fallen foul of marauding Vikings and been impaled on a pagan idol. When this idol was removed from Northye's body, it crumbled to dust in an act of divine intervention which, at once, inspired the Vikings to give up their heathen ways and convert to Christianity, founding the nearby monastery. Unfortunately, it had suffered during the Reformation and was mostly now in ruin. Though a sacred well still survived.

And thrived.

Ahead the children had already gathered in a ragged semi-circle about the platform, waiting impatiently for the priest to take his place. Some of the mothers elbowed their way to the front, tight but animated, keeping watchful eyes on their rabble. The air was sultry and quiet, the insects buzzing in appreciation.

To an impromptu round of applause Father Hadred ascended the wooden platform. It had been dragged out of its year-long storage, dusted down, erected at the holy site and decked lovingly in seasonal flowers. Cissie spotted anemones, sprightly narcissi and forget-me-nots amongst the corn offerings. Someone had added in blood-red tulips which she thought too bold. By Father Hadred's feet she spotted a posy that looked indisputably plastic, a new fashion she deplored. Her neighbour, Ada, was a fan. To have such loveliness all year round, Ada protested, was a gift from God.

Cissie disagreed. Yes, the flowers never faded, but this she saw to be a perversion, a supreme arrogance that pitted itself against Nature. And God.

A couple of the children had crept up to the platform as if to sit on it. Cissie looked around for the mothers, but they did not seem to mind this insolence. The younger generation, she lamented, were ill-disciplined. Rogationtide had favoured them for three years. But this trend could not go on for ever. Sitting on the stage though – it was an afront. She was sure the elders would not approve of such casual attitudes. But they were further back, some blind, others as deaf as the posts which marked out the area.

Father Hadred raised his arms. The gathering fell silent. After a moment the holy man cleared his voice then recited once more the ancient prayer. The villagers became solemn and returned their response: 'We hear you Lord, we will not flinch.'

When the prayer was concluded and all had opened their eyes Father Hadred smiled.

It was time for Mr Heart.

The butcher climbed onto the platform, red-faced and perspiring, dressed like a country squire, holding his silver bucket. When he had settled, Father Hadred turned and, as was traditional, addressed the crowd.

'And so it is that we have come once again to this day. The land has been good to us this year. Let us see if it will be good again.' And he picked up the white surplice and, squinting at his parish, raised it up high.

In the children's ranks excited cries began to bubble. Some jostled.

'Let us see if Mother Nature will ease our way.' And he threw the cloth into the air.

There was not much wind today, yet a light zephyr picked up the fabric and floated it over to the field where it arched up then began to swoon. As soon as the surplice touched the heads of corn, the children were off! Springing loose of their guardians, they raced into the crop.

One was only able to map their progress by the disturbance they made in the tall grass. Though some of the older boys' heads could be seen bobbing over the tops before they ducked down to the ground.

'I've a good feeling about this year,' said a voice next to Cissie. It was Linda from the shoe shop, smiling with straightened lips. Cissie nodded, aware that she had a two-year-old. He was not there, but she could see Linda's eyes moving over the wheat as the children's flitting forms appeared and disappeared, dark flashes in the stems.

Really Cissie should tell her that feelings were worthless on a day like this, but she kept her thoughts to herself and merely said, 'We shall see what we shall see.'

'We've been on a roll,' said Linda. 'None for three year.'

'Which makes it all the more likely,' Cissie retorted and held back a 'tut'.

'Could be worse,' Linda said. 'Could be living in Iders End.' She winked at Cissie. 'That lot are barking.' Then she laughed. 'We'll be all right this year.'

Cissie thought Linda selfish. Rogationtide was not about individuals but about the whole of Northye. One must put aside one's own narrow desires for the greater good.

There was a stirring in the crowd around her. With a cry of delight, Jack Pritt, the farmer's eldest stood up.

'What's he got? Can you see?' asked Linda and she angled her head for a better view.

So soon? Cissie thought and peered at the field. Jack was waving as he returned to the platform, something rusty and thin in his hand.

'It's a fox!' Linda exclaimed and began to clap. 'A fox. I knew it. Didn't I say so,' and she began to laugh.

Cissie thought her reaction inappropriate.

Others clearly did not. A ripple of relief ran through the line of mothers then waved out over the rest of the crowd.

'A fox!' said someone behind her. 'Would you credit it?'

'Fourth time it's provided,' said another.

Cissie, however, felt an unaccountable anger heat her, as if she had been cheated. If no one else could have seen her she might have stamped her foot, but she did not want to be viewed as ungenerous or of having a particular view on the matter. Though it was evident that she did.

Back up on the platform Father Hadred had taken Jack's offering and was now holding it up for all to see. She did not think much of it. The creature had obviously come undone in a trap and not fared well in the early summer sun. It was leached and dried. Parts of its fur detached themselves from the parched skin and fell onto the floor. Not much of a morsel, to be sure. If she had her way, it certainly would not count.

But the priest was accepting.

'And so it is with grace we give thanks for this gift,' he said.

'We hear you Lord,' intoned Cissie along with the rest. 'We will not flinch.'

Hadred nodded and let his hands fall. Smiling he looked to Mr Heart. 'What do you think then?' he asked with a bawdy wink.

Honestly, Cissie thought, where was the sanctity, where was the respect? Hadred was becoming lax in his dotage. They would come undone, she knew it.

The children had returned from the field and gathered once more into their messy formation, mud on their knees and straw in their hair. A few of them started calling 'Yes!' 'Mr Heart!', 'To me, to me!'

'All right then,' said the butcher. He grinned, then with an exaggerated swing he threw the bucket up into the air.

Liquid flew out of it, holly-berry-red, up, up into an arc. In an instant, the children raised their hands and fingers to the blood, opening their mouths to catch some of the precious stuff as it splashed down over the assembly.

'Little savages,' said Linda with a fond smile as the kids swooped down to gather up the stuff. Some had smeared it across their faces, others were licking it from the ground.

'Hmm!' said Cissie and turned to head through the already dispersing crowd. She had had quite enough. 'The year will go fast,' she said, and began to move away.

Already she could hear the band starting up in the village hall. The Joneses would be setting out the cider, the young folk sneaking around the tap trying to catch a nip while their parents' backs were turned.

Yes, the year would be short. But would it be prosperous?

That was the nub.

She could feel the sun biting the skin on her neck, the land seething underneath her feet as she walked.

Denied a proper feast – the flesh and blood of an innocent – deprived this worthy sacrifice, insulted so, it would not take too long for Fortune to turn on its wheel.

Then one desiccated fox would not be enough.

No, not at all.

AFTER THE PARTY
COMES THE BILL

'What's all this about?'

I might as well not bother saying it. There's no one here. C2C. The staff have slunk off early I bet. Christmas Eve and all that.

Don't blame them I suppose – you've got to take advantage of people's good will to get the best out of life, whether that means being creative with your expenses, grabbing a cuddle with the boss's wife, a bit of moonlighting or, in this case, abandoning your train station to sod off down the pub.

Slackers.

Half the lights are out, which does not help things. Got to be illegal? I'm sure Health and Safety will have something to say about leaving passengers on the platform in the dark. I mean, I could fall over something and injure my poor little self. Then it's just a quick call to Accident Lawyers Are Us to instigate action for compensation pertaining to my work-preventing injury and deep emotional distress.

Got a good mind to phone their complaints line now, report the lot of them. That'll undoubtedly give those responsible a very happy new year. Ha ha ha. Serves them right.

Now where's my phone?

Ah, got it.

NO SIGNAL.

What the hell's going on? There's always coverage here.

I can't even see what time it is – screen's not bright enough.

This brand's bloody rubbish. Cost a bomb too.

That's it – Boxing Day I'm marching straight into town, into that phone shop, and I shall not hold back in coming forwards with my views on this piece of tat.

The thought makes me smile and already I'm imagining the expression of the saddo bank-holiday worker, doing it for overtime, when they are duly MADE TO FEEL MY WRATH. Might take a photo. With my phone. Before throwing it in their face. Tee hee.

For a moment the scenario distracts me from my present woe. Then I come to and realise where I am.

That's right – up Fenchurch Street without a paddle.

And it's Christmas sodding Eve.

Bleedin' Norah – you couldn't make it up.

I'm guessing it must be well after midnight now. But I shouldn't have missed the Vomit Comet, as we call the last train.

Let me think – the party went on till eleven. If you can call it that. Not the best Christmas do the world has ever seen. Though when Colin Fennick opened his wallet to get his card out for the tab I was about to make the obligatory comment about moths, but Ralph from sales beat me to it. Fennick had a good laugh and held the card up in the air so I went, 'At least he's managed to get something up, ain't you, Limpdick?'

Should have seen his face, like I was something the cat brought in. Possibly also as I pinched his bird's bum when she come in. She didn't make much fuss about it neither so I reckon she's not getting serviced proper back home.

Anyway I was glad to see that superior grin slip off his sweaty chops. Thought about copping another feel of Mrs Limpdick but got embroiled in some shots down the end of the bar with the postroom lot. Boy did we rack them up. Limpdick'll probably need to remortgage.

Then it was off down the laptop club for a little bit of bump and grind with Tanker Pete, mate of Pots Frischman up Traitor's Gate.

Pete, well he certainly lives up to his name, that one: powers into the club like yer proverbial tank and goes on manoeuvres immediately, if you know what I mean. Had his hands all over one of the Eastern Europeans. And he weren't too gentle neither. Laugh? I really did. Of course security bundled straight over to cool his ardour. Not that the rest of the clientele were bothered about it. Everyone was off their nuts, as they rightly should be come Christmas Eve.

The bird who gave me a dance was all right. Bruises round her neck – looked like fingerprints – and that faraway look I've come to recognise with the girls in there. Spotted a couple of tracks down her arms, so I got no sympathy. She earned a pretty little packet from me: fair exchange I reckon.

Pete bought a gram of Devil's Dandruff from one of her mates. Girl gave us a right grin as she palmed it over. Got to say, I didn't like that look so I took out a tenner and threw it at her feet, just to see her pick it up. They need to know who's master and who's servant in places like that. Funny thing was, she didn't bend down and pick it up. Just winked, without smiling, turned round and buggered off. Suit yerself, I thought and scooped it up. Waste not, want not, is what I say.

Hung around long enough for Pete to chop out some lines, had a couple of very nice big fat ones – thank you very much – then I split and went for the train.

That must put it about what – fifty after midnight when I got here? Not sure. That Colombian marching powder don't arf play havoc with your sense of time.

Mmm, now I'm wondering – could I have dropped off for a moment? I mean, is it actually possible when coked up to the eyeballs? Can't think it would be. But then, how did I end up here with no one else around and the station on some sort of generator or emergency power or something?

Don't make sense.

Rewind: I sat down on the bench here, on the platform. That I do remember. Then … No nothing. Must 'ave blacked out for a minute and only just got back to myself now. Yeah, that works.

So, does that mean I'm locked in? Because there is no way I am spending Christmas Day on this freezing station. Though, actually come to think of it, I ain't that cold. Good.

I sit there for a moment then make a decision. It'll cost a fortune but … taxi it is.

A quick vault across the barriers will see me out of here. I've done that many a time when I've wanted a free ride.

Or maybe I could walk down the tracks a bit and climb over a fence? I can see one a bit further down. Don't look that high.

Hang on. Wait a sodding minute ….

Thank Christ I didn't get on the tracks – there's a train coming.

Uh oh. No lights.

But there's got to be a driver on board. I shall most definitely have words with him to express my profound disappointment with the lack of care regarding customer safety.

To be fair, I would like to see him squirm. I have been well and truly put out. Someone should pay a refund at the very least please. Double it for my inconvenience.

The doors are beeping now.

I'm getting on.

If it goes to the depot I'll get a cab from there. Cheaper than getting one all the way home.

But, good Christ, it's minging in here. The seats are filthy. No one takes pride in their jobs no more. 'Cept for me. I love screwing out the notes, profit and loss, filling in the blanks, being creative. Tax loops, loss recoups. Nothing escapes me and my big round eyes – all the better to see you with, dear.

Still, I shall be adding to my complaint and including some gross misgivings regarding the unsanitary conditions in this carriage. Standards have indeed fallen.

In fact, this is appalling. I take off my raincoat and fold it so I can sit down and not sully the threads of my very expensive new suit.

And then we're off.

Bit of a bumpy start. Perhaps the driver's had a sniff or three of the barmaid's apron? Sozzled for sure. I would be. Hang on, I am. Don't feel it. But of course, I'm forgetting Mr Charlie and his perky party ways.

Bleedin' hell this carriage stinks. And the light – dim, like the station. Though my eyes are starting to adjust and I can see black tarry stains on the seats opposite. Disgusting.

Right, that's it. I'm not staying here. Got to be a cleaner coach further down. So I get to my feet. Mind you – the train ain't half swinging. I have to grab onto a handle on the seat to hold steady. It's got some kind of slime on it. Gross and grosser. The cleaners should be shot. Shoddy work. Without thinking, I wipe my hand on my trousers, then curse. There goes my suit. Another thing to add to my official complaint – dry-cleaning bill.

Someone's in the next carriage. A young bloke. He's as still and as silent as a statue. Balaclava on. But the eyes are alive, intense, darting about in his head. I could be wrong, but his clothes look burnt at the edges. Could be smoking, or it could be my eyes playing up.

Gives me the creeps so I move on.

There's another one up by the window over there. A worried-looking suit, peering out the window into the darkness. Expensive whistle, I can tell. Probably a trader. When they hit the big time them lot don't stay thrifty. I've seen it happen. This one's got a chunk of a watch too. The money's talking. But he's not. He don't look happy neither. I think I recognise him. Don't know where from, mind. Not someone I'd like to party with. But he seems to know me. Or at least he nods like he's sorry or something. A weird nod. Like when you're at a match and it's nearly over and the other side get that last final goal and you know it's game over and catch the eye of a fellow supporter who's a stranger. That kind of nod.

I don't know him but I sort of snicker. When he smiles back I see he's got these yellow pointed canines. I've definitely seen him before but I ain't been in company with him. I remember those teeth.

Don't fancy joining him, so I go down to the next table of four. It's empty. Seats are grimy here too. Definitely moaning about this. I'm going to leave a message on their complaint line now. Might help my claim.

No signal. Still.

Let's try further down the train.

The interconnecting carriage doors open and there's a ropey woman coming through. She's well pale. Hair pulled back in a Croydon face lift. Thin lips. Walks up the aisle and comes at me, a bit glazed, and says, 'Have you seen my kids? I only left them for a moment. Seriously. Just a minute. Maybe ten. No more than that though. I'm so tired. No one listens any more.'

'No love, can't help you there,' I tell her, but I'm thinking, 'You scrag. What time is this to be out with your kids?' Some people got no moral fibre.

She's looking at me with those little piercing eyes and her mouth sucked in tight like an arsehole. 'You're very white,' she says.

And now I'm like 'Have you seen the state of yourself, love?'

For a second her eyes flash with clarity and she does that nod, like the trader did, and says, 'You're bleeding.'

Then she's off again and I can hear her going for the suit. 'Have you seen my kids? I only left them for a minute …'

She won't get no help from him.

I put my hand up to my face but nothing comes off. Crazy loon. Don't know why I believed her anyway. She's off her head.

And so then I'm wondering when we're going to pull in to the next station. Can't see nuffink through the windows. If I cup my hand against it and look through my reflection I can make out shapes on the horizon. But they don't look familiar. By now, we should be on the outskirts of London, but all I see is trees. Big pointy pine ones. Like Christmas trees. But these aren't the type that you'd stick in the living room. These are more like monster plants. Gigantic, at least ten metres high and moving. Weird – it's like they're bending towards the train.

That ain't right.

And that ain't familiar.

We shouldn't be here.

Where are we?

I'll have to get along to the driver and sort it out.

As I'm making my way down the next carriage, which is even sodding darker, the train starts to slow, thank Christ. I'll hop off, walk down the station and get on a cleaner carriage. Probably the quiet coach. The numpties in there usually keep themselves to themselves. Don't mess things up. I'll get in and put my feet up. Try and get a bit of kip.

Picking up speed again.

I'll have to go down the carriages.

But the floor's not even. It's starting to slope: we're going downhill.

Before I reach the internal doors there's a sudden clang and a change in the air, like the pressure's sucked out. Must be in a tunnel.

This is definitely not my route.

Hard to walk, but I manage to wobble down to the next set of doors.

They're not the sliding sort, like the rest. More like an old train's, with wooden frames and a greasy window. The doorknob's metal, brass or something, but friggin' hot. I have to use the sleeve of my jacket. Jesus. But I manage to open it and get in.

Now this coach is virtually black. My stomach does a massive friggin' flip when I see dark wisps of smoke or some shit hanging in the air. Is there a fire? Maybe someone's 'aving a fag. I can't see. There's no overhead lighting, just these flickering lights on the sides: candle bulbs so grubby they don't give off hardly any glow at all.

And I can hear things moving under seats, slithering and scuttling across the floor. Wouldn't surprise me if this coach had rats. The stench is well rank.

There's something at the end that's giving off a bit of light: a neon sign. Looks out of place on this part of the train. More like something on an arcade game: reddish, blinking.

When I'm only a few feet away it flashes brightly for a moment. Then an LED ticker-tape message board comes on. Good. Hopefully it'll have our destination come up on it soon.

As the little red lights begin to appear on the screen I see there's someone sitting on the seat underneath it. And, well blow me, if it's not Tanker Pete!

I'm glad to see the old sod, I can tell you. Life at last!

So as I shuffle forward I go 'Oi oi saveloy.' He likes all the bantz.

But not this time. There's something that's not right with him. In the shadows he looks as murky as sin. Got a right face on him. His eyes are unfocussed, like the pupils are spinning and tight. When he looks up I see he's got a massive sodding nosebleed. In this light it looks as thick as gravy and just as lumpy and brown.

'Pete, me old china, what you doing on here then? And mate, you know your nose …'

He sees it's me and for a moment he brightens. At bloody last, the sour git. Then he starts chortling, a nasty spiteful laugh, the kind that's not meant to be joined in with. When he stops and breathes, a slow rasping wheeze comes over him. He steadies himself and says 'Nose? Yeah, I know,' and dabs at his left nostril. 'I don't think it's ever going to stop.'

And I say, 'Hang about, I've got a tissue somewhere.'

But he goes, 'Doesn't matter. I've tried.' Then he says. 'You're bleeding too.'

And I put my hand to my face and as it comes away I clock that there's darkish watery stuff on it and I think, why didn't I see that before? And I try to rub it with my sleeve, but he's right – it's not doing any good. Nothing is stemming the flow.

'What's this all about?' I go.

'They laced it,' he says, matter-of-fact like, and shrugs. 'Harsh, if you ask me.' Then he turns back and looks out the window. 'It ain't ever going to stop.'

'Oh come on, mate. Chin chin. It's Christmas,' I say trying to jolly him up. 'What you doing on this train anyway? You go North, don't cha?'

That gets him and he comes back to me. 'For gawd's sake. You ain't got it, 'ave yer?'

Now I'm starting to get testy. Wouldn't kick a mate while he's bleeding. Unless pushed.

'Always a bit slow on the take-up.' Pete laughs again. 'Have you walked down the train?'

I nod with my chin pointed out, like I'm saying, 'Yeah, so?'

'Recognise anyone?'

'Should I?'

He tuts at me. 'Thick.'

And now I'm ready to smack him one, mate or no.

But he goes: 'That geezer back in carriage one – Gary Franklin, innit. Hedge fund manager and embezzler.'

And the name stops me. Rings a bell somewhere, but it's not a nice sound that it's making.

And then it's coming to me out of the blackness. That's right, come to mention it, I've got him now. Then another thought lands. 'Oh yeah. What's he doing on here? Heard he got taken out by some of the people he did business with. They didn't appreciate his "commission", if I recall?'

But Pete doesn't answer that. He says, 'The woman looking for her kids, not familiar?'

I shake my head and see little drops of blood fling themselves onto the floor between our shoes. I don't recognise her at all. A scuttling thing darts across the floor and I shift my feet.

Pete sniffs, a gurgling snotty blood-filled snort. 'Just got done for killing them. Smothered 'em with a pillow in their sleep.'

Now I remember. But that doesn't work out. 'But she done herself in?' I can hear my voice go up at the end, uncertainty crowding in. 'How can she …?'

'Work it out,' says Pete but his voice is no longer firm. 'There's only one destination on this route,' he says and nods at the flashing LED sign. 'That will give you a clue. Does what it says on the tin.'

And I turn and read it, and as I do I hear a voice which is mine, start to groan.

Train terminating.

THE OVER-WINTER
HARROWING OF
CONSTANCE HEARST

The discovery of Constance Hearst's body occasioned a clamour of consternation in Adder's Fork. Of course, any corpse would provoke a reaction from the community in which he or she was found. Death, as we know, is a transitional phase of life that many wish to ignore. Through no fault of their own. It is but a part of the human condition to view one's demise with trepidation and fear. And learning of other's journeys across the Styx to the Land of the Dead often prompts reflections upon the soul and one's own mortal fragility.

However, the circumstances of this unfortunate tragedy were so very disturbing, they invaded the imagination of the public. Realising they were on to a good thing, the case was picked up by the national papers. Headlines appeared, lurid and bold. One, in particular, persisted in the minds of its readers and thus became attached to the investigation so that even the assigned officers began to refer to their work as The Harrowing of Constance Hearst. Or The Harrowing, for short. It was a fitting title.

There were three reasons why.

First, the manner in which Miss Hearst was found was peculiar in the extreme. The county had borne the brunt of bad weather during that bitter winter and there had been a prolonged period of snowfall. Strong winds had whirled the flakes in huge cyclones that had wrapped around trees and bushes and sprayed white grains over everything. Adder's Fork, the little village at the centre of the drama, had come off worse than those surrounding. Large drifts were not uncommon in that part of Essex, and the church being at a fork in the road, and by some quirk of geography on a slight elevation, meant that the graveyard was often engulfed by several large white mounds, under which one might traditionally find the nativity figures that had been proudly displayed in the village every Christmas for eons.

It was not until early February when the thaw began, that the snow and ice commenced its recession and gave up its unexpected horror. For, beside St

Michaels and All Angels, partly concealed behind the large bent elm that looked as if its branches had been brushed back neatly and parted for Sunday best, stood the corpse of Constance Hearst. Still frozen, her features assumed an expression of extreme surprise.

Even little Johnnie Acton, from Snakes Lane Farm, who first glimpsed her hat peeking from the melting mound, remarked, 'I realised it was a lady there. So I come over and asked her if she was all right. But she was so fixed on something ahead, I thought she hadn't heard me and took a gander at where she was looking. Turns out – the Seven Stars. I said, "What's caught you over there, Mrs?" to see if she was going to tell me what amazed her so. When she didn't answer I went and poked. Stiff as a board, she was. Put the frighteners up me straight off, so that's when I got us the vicar. To let 'im know she was here.'

A wise and indeed sensible move. For when the Reverend Benthal returned with Johnnie, he bade the boy run to the police box and send up the alarm. Unlike the young lad, Benthal had, you see, observed the second dastardly reason the story lives on in the minds of the villagers: Constance Hearst's throat had been cut from ear to ear. The blood had frozen and, as the reverend was to describe later in court, it 'could almost be mistaken for a necklace made of ruby stalactites. Quite the dress piece, if one didn't know.'

Inspector George LeGrand of Litchenfield Police, an officer of both distinguished record and sterling reputation, was despatched with immediate effect and arrived in the village that very evening.

The defrosting cadaver had been laid upon the table in the rectory kitchen to which he was directed. Upon arrival the inspector was taken forthwith to the makeshift morgue by the Benthals' housekeeper. Here he made the acquaintance of the reverend from whom he secured the details of the discovery.

When asked if the identity of the deceased was known, the Reverend immediately referred the inspector to a locket found upon the damaged neck. It bore an image of the dead woman and another, presumably her sister, for she looked not much younger. In addition, the names Constance and Prudence Hearst were engraved within.

When LeGrand's sergeant, one Peter Brown, appeared, he was required to make enquiries as to the residence of these certain Hearst sisters while the inspector continued to examine the body.

The Reverend Benthal pointed to the quality of the cloak the deceased had been wearing. Hung up on a hook in the pantry, it proved to have been woven from French velvet and although still wet, the men could see that the colour had not faded and the condition was excellent.

'She must have been a woman of good standing,' remarked LeGrand.

'But not from round here,' the reverend confirmed. 'As far as I am aware, all such ladies of the parish are well and present. She has come from further afield.'

A little later, when they were taking tea in the library, Sergeant Brown returned with information pertaining to the residence of the Hearst sisters, which he had learnt was in a village, Fobbing End, north of Chelmsford.

With it being a matter of urgency, and not wishing the surviving Hearst sister to learn of the demise of her sibling through tittle-tattle, the inspector immediately commanded a carriage and issued to Fobbing Hall, the Hearst house.

It was here that LeGrand happened on the third most perplexing aspect of the crime.

Shown into the drawing room he found Prudence sitting by the fire with her needlework. In her thirties, with unfussy dress and a comportment that suggested she would not brook any nonsense, she enquired as to the nature of his visit. Without any further ado LeGrand broke the tragic news of the death. He had done this many times and had already forewarned the maid to bring brandy. However, Prudence did not shriek or swoon. She merely stared at him with an open mouth. Assuming she may be imbecilic, the inspector began again with his grim report, this time in a slower more simplistic manner. In this, however, he was fortunately interrupted. For just as he was to impart, once again, the news of her sister's demise, in walked Constance Hearst.

'Hello,' said the deceased. 'I was told we had company.'

Now it was LeGrand's turn to be dumbfounded.

The woman who appeared in the drawing room was the very spit of the girl on the table in the rectory. Her hair was an identical russet brown, her stature and size similar. The eyes too were the same shape. Of the colour he could not tell: the pall of death had descended upon the corpse before he was able to discern them. The only differences he could detect were that this woman was a fraction older, perhaps in her late twenties. And she was alive.

Very much so. Her eyes dancing with fire. Fully animate.

'You look as if you've seen a ghost, Inspector,' said Constance Hearst.

'My dear woman, I think I have,' he replied, and with that he staggered to a fine armchair and let his weight fall therein.

The brandy, which arrived with the maid, was quickly poured, but it was to the inspector it was most urgently administered.

After a few minutes of great confusion LeGrand was able to communicate to the sisters some of the events of the day.

When he had finished, Constance said, 'Well, I can assure you, inspector, that I am not yet extinct. I don't know who you have upon the table in the Adder's Fork rectory, but it is not me.'

'I can vouch for my sister,' added Prudence, much concerned. 'We have not gone out for days. The weather has been treacherous and we have taken good care to keep our household safe.'

LeGrand agreed that it was a most perplexing affair and soon took to his feet. 'Please direct me to the nearest house with a telephone,' he said. 'I must speak to my sergeant.'

Fortunately, such a device had been recently installed in the Hearst household so without delay LeGrand was able to make contact with his sergeant who informed him that the body had been taken to the Litchenfield mortuary.

Returning to the drawing room, he informed the sisters of the development and asked if one of them would be so good as to accompany him to Litchenfield on the morrow to regard the deceased with a view to ascertaining her identity.

'We think it may be Bella,' Constance informed him.

'Cartwright,' Prudence added. 'She was our lady's maid.'

'Reliable for years,' Constance explained. 'Although a change came over her and we had to let her go.'

'When was that?' LeGrand asked.

Constance looked at her sister. 'It was when the nights turned cold and short, wasn't it, Pru?'

Prudence nodded and said with absolute conviction, 'She left on December the first. I opened the first door of the advent calendar – it revealed a picture of a happy household decorating a Christmas tree. I remember feeling it to be intensely ironic. Our home was in turmoil. Bella was well liked. Not everyone agreed with our decision. Though we felt we had little choice, we were still sad to see her go.'

'If only she had stopped …' Constance muttered.

'What occasioned her dismissal?' LeGrand addressed the elder sister, who at this present moment, appeared to have more focus.

Prudence sniffed and rubbed her hands together. 'Not that we would want to cast aspersions on her good character,' Constance, who he had noticed was very sprightly and lithe, brought up a stool and sat by him. 'It was brought to our notice,' she began, 'that a few personal items had disappeared.'

'A locket?' asked LeGrand and both sisters gasped.

'But how could you know?' asked Prudence.

'It was how we identified you,' LeGrand told them. 'Or at least how I came to be here imparting the news of your demise to poor Miss Hearst. Bella was wearing it.'

'But whatever could she have been doing in Adder's Fork?' asked Constance.

Her older sister sighed. 'And what could possibly occasion her murder?'

To that, none could provide an answer.

It was agreed that the next day Constance, who appeared the more willing of the two, would accompany the inspector to Litchenfield and set about the grim task of identifying the corpse. Until then their new maid was to make up a bed in the spare room and LeGrand was invited to keep the spinsters company overnight – a task he did not mind. And, so they told him, neither did they have any objections, being so deprived of male company over winter in the country.

The evening passed enjoyably. At dinner, the two ladies chatted with much animation about the deterioration in Bella Cartwright's performance. The resemblance to Constance had been noted but not overdone, until summer. Earlier that year an elderly bachelor uncle had passed away and left the Hearst sisters a brand new motorcar and something of a small fortune in jewellery and dividends. Commonly thrifty by nature, the two discussed splashing out on a rare treat. A trip to Paris to freshen their wardrobes with some haute couture and fabrics for day wear was decided upon. After which Constance, being of roughly the same build and height as Bella, gave her maid a number of her old gowns.

It was at a summer party at the rectory that Bella, arriving before the sisters in one of Constance's old dresses, had been taken for the younger Miss Hearst. Much fun was made of the mistake and the story was retold, at first, with gaiety.

Prudence suddenly set down her spoon with a clang. They were on dessert. 'It wasn't long after that she bobbed her hair.'

'Oh,' said Constance, her face losing its glow. 'Yes. I see.'

But LeGrand didn't. 'How is that of relevance?'

Constance turned to him and smiled. 'The hair fashion was quite the rage in Paris. We visited a coiffeur and I had mine cut short.' She moved her hand back and forth across her jawline, which was lean and pleasingly curved, to indicate the length.

LeGrand eyed her hair, which was piled up upon her head. He could picture her with a short cut and imagined it might look rather mischievous, if not most certainly fetching.

Self-conscious now, she tucked back an errant lock of hair. Her ears, LeGrand noticed, were small, alabaster and shell-like.

'Oh …' Constance broadened her smile, checking where his gaze fell. 'It's grown. But Prudence is right, in summer Bella copied my style. The likeness, the similarity in features, became more noticeable.' Then she too let her hands drop to the table. 'Goodness,' she said, eyes becoming rounder. 'Do you think that might have had something to do with … with … her …?' She let the sentence tail off.

An image of the dead woman dripping on the rectory table flashed over LeGrand's mind. Eager to preserve the most gracious lady from pain and such horror, LeGrand cut in. 'No, no. Of course it didn't.'

But his mind was ticking over: of course it did.

The next day was gloomy. Constance's mood was not as ebullient as the night before, although she tried to inject her voice with energy and make small talk as they powered down the narrow lanes and byroads of Fobbing End on to the city of Litchenfield. The purpose of their visit weighed upon them, wrapping both with tension like an invisible shroud.

LeGrand, whilst happy to be in the company of Constance Hearst, was concerned as to the younger sister's reaction when he exposed her to the cadaver. Although his mother had instilled him with more respect for the fairer sex than was perhaps appropriate for a serving officer of the law, melodramas made him queasy. He was more comfortable with an efficient suppression of emotion and was admiring of restraint and discipline.

On the whole Constance appeared composed, however, he continued to worry how the presence of death might affect her. Fortunately, or perhaps not so, he soon became distracted by the hectic driving style with which she manoeuvred her late uncle's car. He had been a tall man and several cushions were required to favour Constance with enough height to see through the windscreen. Turning corners often dislodged some of the elevating pads and resulted in erratic tugs on the steering wheel, which sent the vehicle motoring towards the hedgerows. Constance, however, in all except one case where they went through the hedge and back again, managed to control the beast. They arrived at Litchenfield morgue intact and before the low sun had reached its winter zenith.

As it was, LeGrand's fears failed to materialise for Constance, although paler than he had seen her, merely confirmed the identity of her lady's maid, Bella Cartwright, with a nod. Pointing to the navy cloak laid out on the table next to the unfortunate wretch, she added, 'That's mine. It disappeared when Bella left. We chose not to pursue the matter. She was already much distressed.'

Although he did not approve of such a lapse, the action or lack of therein, in a strange illogical manner further elevated his approbation and growing regard in respect of Constance's character. She was charitable too, he saw.

Later, in a small office, over a freshly brewed cup of Indian tea, Constance shared a further insight.

'It was after she picked up the cloak from town that the trouble began,' she ruminated, eyes glassy with uneasy remembrance.

'Trouble?' LeGrand enquired.

'I could put it down to that day in fact,' Constance nodded. 'We had asked her to go to the post office here to pick up that cloak. I had the measurements taken in Paris, but the outfitters were behind with their orders and agreed to send it on. The garment took several months to arrive. When it did, myself and Prudence were occupied with preparing the house for our cousin's visit, so we despatched Bella to collect it. She took a carriage and was some time. We didn't really notice how long until night fell, and we grew worried. However, she turned up at around eight o'clock that night with some excuse that did not seem credible. Though we were more concerned with entertaining by that hour. She was very apologetic.'

LeGrand put down his tea. 'Where was she to collect it from?'

'The central post office,' Constance replied.

'Then we should go there at once and see what they have to say,' LeGrand said. 'Or I should.'

But Constance was happy enough to accompany the man of the law.

By great coincidence the clerk who had served Bella Cartwright was on duty. And he remembered the incident well enough.

'There were customs dues to be paid. It had come from France,' he recalled.

'Do you have a record of the package?' LeGrand asked.

The clerk nodded. 'I will have to look in the office. But it will be there. Please wait.' And he drew down the blind.

While they waited LeGrand noticed that his companion's countenance had changed. Her eyes were downcast and their customary sparkle had left her eyes.

'Would you like to sit down, Miss Hearst?' he asked.

She shook her head and said, 'You may call me Constance. I think we have gone through enough to warrant a waiving of formalities.' And then she placed her hand on his arm, below the elbow, above the wrist. He felt it there, firm and warm, showering sparks like a comet as it moved minutely. For a moment he could not breathe.

'I am besieged by guilt,' she said, unaware of the avalanche of feelings in the man standing close to her, which had been unleashed by her light touch.

'If we had not let Bella go, then she may well still be alive.'

Mastering his vocal cords, the inspector drew breath. 'Constance,' he said, enjoying the luxury of her name on his tongue. 'Constance, you cannot know that to be true.' Then, unthinkingly he placed his hand over hers, still smouldering on his forearm. 'I should not have taken you to the mortuary, I fear.'

He felt her fingers twitch underneath his palm and again, a bolt of electricity tore up his arm.

Constance's eyes flashed. 'I will not have you think me weak, sir. I may be a woman, but you should understand: my father had no sons. He raised both Prudence and I to be stronger and more courageous, more principled than most good men you will find.'

Her speech warmed him and out of nowhere he found a deep and fond smile spreading over his face. 'I have no doubt of that. It is very much in evidence.'

When Constance looked into his face, her frown too was replaced by a smile, and the air between them filled with a sweet nectar invisible to none other.

The blind squeaked as it was hoisted. The sound instantly snapped Constance and LeGrand out of their fleeting reverie. Both stepped quickly away from each other. Constance blushed as if caught in an act of intimacy.

The moment moved on.

'I have it here,' said the clerk, leaning over the counter with a docket. 'It was October the fifteenth. In fact, I remember it well. It was nearly three weeks before Guy Fawkes night and yet some of the urchins had their dummy out and were begging for pennies. In fact, the young lady tripped on the gang, who had settled very naughtily by our door. Usually,' he confided in the inspector, 'we take no brook with such behaviour, but this lot had slipped in unnoticed.'

'Quite, quite,' said the inspector, who had composed himself, though he remained intensely aware of the nearness of Miss Hearst.

'I went to shoo them out,' the clerk continued. 'The lady dropped the package. Of course, I would have assisted, but there was a man. He had been waiting in line and went to her assistance and picked it up. He remarked upon the postmark. They had some discussion.'

'Do you remember what he said?' LeGrand asked with impatience, his sense of detection tingling.

'I believe,' said the clerk. 'It was something along the lines of "A French dress, Mrs Hearst?"'

'And what did she say?' exclaimed Constance. 'Did she put him right on that?'

'Oh yes,' said the clerk. 'She did indeed. She told him, "It is *Miss* Hearst."'

Constance's hand flew to her mouth. 'But she had no right to let him think that …'

Inspector LeGrand motioned for her to be silent.

Although the blood rose to her cheeks, she reluctantly obeyed.

The clerk did not notice the frisson that had passed between them and continued. 'I have a notion that the young man suggested they take tea somewhere. It was a chill day and Miss Hearst's hands were without gloves. He insisted they go somewhere to warm them.'

'Most strange,' remarked Constance when they had removed outside. 'Why did she not apprise him of who she was?'

'That one I'm sure is easy to guess,' said LeGrand, offering her an arm. 'She simply didn't want to.'

'But …' said Constance and threaded her arm through the inspector's. 'But why?'

LeGrand did not answer, for his mind was occupied by the manifestation of a picture that was assembling. 'The coachman,' he said then. 'May I speak with him?'

Miss Hearst nodded. 'But he is not one of our staff. I borrowed the carriage from Mr Scruton who has the next farm over. We were using the motorcar that weekend.'

'Mmm,' cogitated LeGrand. 'Is his house installed with a telephone?'

'No,' said Constance. 'But I can take you to him and you may stay over again if it becomes too late.'

And so, the arrangement being pleasing to both parties, they quickly departed once more for Fobbing End.

After relaying the details of the grim situation, Farmer Scruton, an amiable fellow, was happy to volunteer the services of his coachman and groom. Though the latter was rather less affable. In fact, LeGrand thought Harry Lewis taciturn and reluctant to speak. Although, as their conversation bore on, he became more convinced that the coachman merely disliked the company of others. The inspector could imagine the sullen fellow sitting atop the carriage guarding its occupants like a stone gargoyle. Though he became more noticeably animated when he remembered Bella and the afternoon in question.

'Yes,' he said, shaking a finger at LeGrand. 'She went awf to some hostelry.'

'Alone?'

'No,' he shook his head. 'With a man. Young chap.'

'Did you get a look at him?'

The felt hat on Lewis's head wobbled as he shook it back and forth. 'Was dark by then.' And shortly, a memory awoke in his head and brightened his eyes. 'Ah, hang about. Come to think of it when she got back into the carriage, later, she asked me about Parnell de Vere?'

'Mmm,' remarked Farmer Scruton. 'That's a thing. Inspector, you said that the corpse was found in Adder's Fork?'

'That's right.' LeGrand said.

'That is also where Parnell de Vere resides. Howlet Manor, indeed.'

'Is it?' LeGrand ventured. 'And what did you tell Bella Cartwright about the gentleman in question?' he asked Lewis.

'The same as Master Scruton,' replied the coachman. 'That he was one of the de Vere's of Adder's Fork. I don't know much more than that. Never been concerned with county folk.'

Constance Hearst was rather more interested than Mr Scruton's groom-cum-coachman. In fact, the lady confided in Inspector LeGrand over supper that night that on several occasions she had been in the company of the young de Vere heir.

Parnell de Vere was, she believed, a 'rather dashing young man'.

LeGrand found himself disconcerted by the reaction of his own face, which began to heat under his whiskers. In a gauche manoeuvre he tried to disguise the crimson spread by stroking out his full moustache. He was unsure, however, if he had acted quickly enough, for Constance spoke up in a squeaky voice.

'Far too young to interest me of course,' she said then laughed very loudly.

Prudence, who that evening was wearing trousers, joined her sister with hearty guffaws. LeGrand had the notion that they had both sensed his discomfort. Although of respectable tradesman stock, he was fully aware he was their social and economic inferior and had no business entertaining thoughts that may or may not pertain to romance, involuntary or not.

'Well,' he made himself speak in a firm and efficient manner, quite at odds with the sea of feeling roiling within his interior landscape. 'I shall return to the village on the morrow and find out for myself.'

'An excellent plan,' said Prudence and moved on swiftly. 'Did we say, we had a call from a correspondent this afternoon?'

LeGrand expressed his surprise, grateful for the change in subject.

'They wanted to speak to Constance, of course.' Prudence nodded at her sister.

Constance, whose complexion had also become rosier, sighed. 'Yes, for a daily national. The news of the misidentification has got out, it seems.'

'Already,' LeGrand muttered, more to himself than the ladies. 'Do you know which publication? It would work to our advantage to keep this matter private for the moment.'

'*The Times,*' Constance informed him. 'You were upstairs in the spare room when I took the call. The reporter asked me if I felt it "harrowing", as he put it. Harrowing. That was the word that he used. It most unsettled me. I told him to call again in a few days. I am not inclined at present to answer enquiries.'

LeGrand lightened. 'That could work in our favour. Perhaps we can tempt them into silence with the promise of an interview exclusively when you are, of course, ready?'

But Constance did not reply. She was looking into her plate.

'He asked me my marital status,' she said and looked up, tensed across the brow. 'And do you know what? I find that "harrowing". That a woman may be judged and represented in terms of her relationship to a man.'

Across the table Prudence clapped her hands. 'Hear, hear.'

'Why …' continued Constance, raising her face. Disconcertingly she appeared to be addressing the question to LeGrand. 'Why is it of any matter whether I am married or betrothed? I am unmarried as it goes, but what purpose does it serve to tell all and sundry? Is it a matter of public interest?' The anger in her voice was unmistakable.

'Certainly it should not be!' Prudence exclaimed.

LeGrand, who had wished to enquire as to why such women of many attributes, good standing in society and so financially well-endowed might remain spinsters, fell silent. For once he was unsure of how to respond.

Perhaps the sisters sensed this because Constance suddenly declared, 'Prudence and I have all that we need. In our experience, men have not enriched our lives.'

The elder sister scoffed. 'Quite the opposite,' she said.

At a loss, LeGrand bit his tongue.

Arising early the following day and, having previously sought permission from the sisters, the inspector made two telephone calls. The first was to his contact in Fleet Street who agreed to approach the daily newspaper editors about the necessary discretion that should be used regarding the case. He also promised to speak with *The Times* about an exclusive, pending their sensitive handling of the information gleaned so far.

The second call was to Sergeant Brown. The inspector informed him of the developments and requested he commandeer a vehicle and meet him at Howlet Manor. Once arrangements had thus been put in place LeGrand made haste to Adder's Fork.

His journey was speedy and as such he arrived at the manor in good time.

Once announced, LeGrand was escorted to the day room where he found the current lord of the manor.

In a place like Adder's Fork such news spread as quickly as the blush on LeGrand's face the night before, and so it was of no surprise that Lord de Vere was well acquainted with the rudimentary facts pertaining to the grim discovery made two days before. He did appear, however, to lack the knowledge that Miss Constance Hearst of Fobbing End was very much alive.

'I am much concerned that a crime of such violent nature as this has been committed in my village,' he told the inspector in a baritone that reminded LeGrand of the grandfather clock that had lived in the hall of the house where he had grown up. The lord was as tall as the timepiece and similarly sonorous. 'And I am of course prepared to offer any assistance and resources that may help in bringing the culprit to justice.'

The good lord's eyes bulged, however, when the inspector informed him that his first request was to speak with his eldest son. After a moment Lord de Vere stood so absolutely still that the inspector questioned if he had forgotten he was there. Then the older man breathed out a long heavy sigh, his face ashen, and said, 'Yes of course. I will ask Jenkins to send him down immediately.'

The inspector almost felt sorry for the man.

As soon as he entered the day room LeGrand could see why women described him as dashing. Parnell de Vere was a good six feet tall and of athletic build. His hair was dark and shining and he wore a full moustache, which the inspector felt a trifle immoderate. Though aside from that there was something distinctly feminine about the young man's features – the lips were as pink as peonies, the eyes a startling blue – and there persisted around the fellow the air of a cad.

Introduced by his father, Parnell gave the inspector an exaggerated, foppish bow, and asked how he might assist the police.

LeGrand immediately requested an account of de Vere's whereabouts on October the fifteenth of the previous year.

Parnell shook his head.

His father's expression grew darker.

'Goodness,' said the young man. 'I wouldn't have a clue.'

At this the lord tutted and with great irritation bellowed, 'All that money spent on a top-class education and you can't keep a single fact in that head of yours. Really Parnell.'

The boy's bluster deserted him and he returned his father's gaze with wide eyes. 'Well, can you? It's a long time ago.'

De Vere Senior turned to LeGrand and apologised. 'I'm sorry Inspector. The boy's head resembles a sieve. He was in Italy during September and October, doing a tour of Tuscany, Florence, then Rome.'

'Oh yes!' Parnell grinned. 'I had aspirations to be an artist.'

'And now?' asked his father.

'It didn't turn out for me. I still don't know. These things take time.'

LeGrand was developing a dislike for the young man and more and more sympathy for his father. 'And you have witnesses who can attest to this?'

'Oh yes,' said Parnell. 'We spent the second and third week at Bunny Tottridge's villa outside Lucca. There was half a dozen of us. An absolutely terrific blast.'

'I can give you Wilfred Tottridge – Bunny's – address,' his father volunteered. 'The family should be in Sussex at the moment.' He called the butler for paper and a pen and presently wrote down the information for LeGrand.

'Very well, you have been most helpful.' The inspector read the address. All seemed in order and he was about to leave to confirm the younger de Vere's whereabouts when his sergeant was announced.

'Excuse me.' LeGrand bowed and quickly withdrew.

In the hall he found Sergeant Brown in a state of mild excitement.

'Well I hope you've got more to report than me,' said LeGrand. 'This one's a dead end, if you'll forgive the pun.'

'Oh yes, indeed, sir. I think you'll be pleased to hear this,' came the response. 'A woman has come forward from the village of Haven, not far from here.'

'Oh yes,' said LeGrand.

'She says her lodger was Constance Hearst.'

The boarding house was not the kind of dwelling where one might expect to find such an elegant woman as the younger Miss Hearst. Of course, ordinarily one would not, but Mrs Stains did not know that. The landlady was a mole-like creature with dirty grey hair pulled back tight into a scraggy tail and huge round spectacles that made her eyes appear as big as saucers. They did not seem to improve her eyesight, however, as she was compelled to come very close to the inspector when she spoke about the mysterious tenant. He could smell her keenly. She did not wash often.

'And she did not settle the rent neither,' Mrs Stains said and eyed the inspector hungrily.

'We may be able to help with a donation in that regard? Where are her effects?' LeGrand made sure the landlady understood one would not come without the other.

Mrs Stains hobbled over to a sideboard and opened a drawer. Bending, she collected the meagre remains of Bella Cartwright's earthly belongings.

On examination the sergeant and his guvnor

found a few threadbare garments, three rather more luxurious robes, some underwear, a shawl, papers and one envelope addressed to a 'Constant Hearse', which LeGrand found ominous and depressing in equal measure.

'We will take these back to the station,' he told the old woman and palmed her off with a few shillings. She accepted the money but grumbled to herself.

'Back to Litchenfield then, guv?' Sergeant Brown suggested as they left. LeGrand shook his head.

'My belly tells me it's time for lunch. Let us repair to the local hostelry.'

Sergeant Brown was in full agreement and within the hour they found themselves settled at a pleasant inn, the Ship and Piper.

They ate hastily. Being younger, quicker and hungrier, Sergeant Brown, the first to finish his meal, asked, 'Shall I read the letter then, sir?'

Receiving permission he rummaged in the hessian sack, which contained the pathetic remnants of a sad life cut short too soon, and withdrew the envelope. Holding it up to the window for illumination, he began to read.

'*Dear Bella,*' he said. '*I am not sure why I must address this to another name, but I know you have your reasons.*' He looked up to LeGrand. 'Spelt "raisons".'

Brown rolled his eyes, but LeGrand said nothing. This misspelling intensified the dismal feeling within him that was far closer to pity than scorn.

'*But I am gladdened to hear,*' the sergeant continued, '*that there has been an improvement in your situation. It is a shame that the sisters moved away, but the times are hard. The house was big and if they could not afford it, tis understandable.*' Brown glanced at LeGrand. 'They have written "tis". That's not my abbreviation sir.'

'Right you are,' said LeGrand drawing in a full lung of air. The sergeant was beginning to irritate him. 'Go on, go on.' He rotated his hand in a circular motion, which communicated some of his internal friction to his junior, who knew his boss well enough to get straight to it.

He cleared his throat. '*We must count our blessings when we have them. And you must count yours. This Parnell fella sounds like a catch. Congratulations on your engagement, dear. We look forward to meeting him. When will you bring him up?*'

At these last words LeGrand winced.

Sergeant Brown continued at full speed.

'*Betty is doing well at school and Cecil has gained an apprenticeship at the mill, so we are not so bad ourselves. The weather has not been good but with*

Cecil's extra money we have been getting more coal.' He ceased his narration, eyes roaming silently over the remaining lines. 'More domestic detail,' he surmised.

'Is there a name or address?' LeGrand asked.

'It's signed "Mother".'

LeGrand sighed and rubbed his forehead.

Even Peter Brown seemed to have lost some of his verve now. 'The address is in Pickering, Yorkshire.'

'We must get word to her, then. The mother,' LeGrand mumbled. 'As soon as we have cleared this mess up.'

Folding the letter back, Sergeant Brown fixed him with a stare, his eyes, which were not large, had contracted to two sharp flinty points. LeGrand found himself admiring what he fathomed within – a quick and steely intellect and unflinching perception. 'So Parnell de Vere is mentioned again …' Brown said.

'Yes,' agreed the inspector, impressed by his junior's courage. Not everyone was prepared to point their finger at the most powerful family in the district. 'Can you get someone onto verifying de Vere's alibi? If there is no telephone here I noted a police box as we came into the village.' He handed him the sheet of paper with Bunny Tottridge's details.

Sergeant Brown rolled his eyes. 'Bunny!'

'I believe it a nickname. He is Wilfred Tottridge.'

'Wilfred is a perfectly good name. Why use another?' Brown shook his head. 'Bunny indeed!' He rose. 'This is a most twisting and perplexing case.'

'It is,' agreed LeGrand. Yet even as he spoke, his sergeant's words echoed in his brain: some sort of idea was sliding into place.

As it was, the Ship and Piper had been recently installed with a telephone and Sergeant Brown was able to crank up the wheels of communication between the Litchenfield Constabulary and their cousins in Sussex. Arriving back at the table a mere twenty minutes later, the sergeant was full of a curious energy.

'Well, that's all in hand,' he said. 'It seems you have had a visitor at the station today, sir,' Brown could not vanquish the smile from his face. 'Miss Hearst the younger has been in.'

'Oh really?' LeGrand straightened at once. 'And?'

'She has asked you to call her on her telephone as soon as is feasible.'

Attempting to represent an air of weary reluctance, the speed with which the senior man jumped to his feet conveyed an entirely different emotion, not lost on his junior.

Without further ado he commandeered the handset and asked the operator to connect him to the house in Fobbing End. He found himself ridiculously elevated to hear Constance's voice on the other end, despite an erratic connection.

'I can't be too long,' Constance told him through heavy static blasts. Her voice was breathy yet still bright. 'We're just off to see *Hamlet* at the Alhambra, but I thought you should know: my solicitor has been contacted by another practising local lawman – who informed him that he is to execute the terms of my will!'

'Your will?' LeGrand frowned heavily. 'And who is this man?'

'Grace and Sons on Old Moulsham Street, Litchenfield. He has reported that in this will I have made my estate over to my fiancé!'

'Leave it to me,' LeGrand said, privately impressed by the authority in his voice. 'I will see them at once.'

'This man, my fiancé, *the* fiancé, he is to meet with the lawyers at their offices on Monday. Can you come to the house tomorrow? I can explain more then.'

LeGrand, of course, assented.

Mr Grace was to be found enjoying a decent supper of veal and potatoes in a sizeable dwelling in a highly desirable suburb of Litchenfield not far from Old Moulsham Street. Clearly displeased at the interruption, the solicitor sighed and then greeted them with an air of expectant wariness.

'This is about the will of Constance Hearst?' he asked, leading them into a private room away from the inquisitive eyes of his family.

The small parlour was wood panelled and warm, which LeGrand gave thanks for. The journey in an open-top vehicle had been … draughty.

Mr Grace directed them to a pair of seats around a mahogany desk, which the two well-travelled officers of the law readily accepted.

'The fact of the matter,' said Mr Grace at once, 'is that no wrongdoing can be attributed to my part in this.'

Sergeant Brown began to speak, but LeGrand halted him. 'How so?'

'I was presented with Miss Constance Hearst and merely carried out her wishes. She appeared to be under no duress about the new will. She was insistent that she should sign over her estate to de Vere, on the event of her death. I duly obliged. I am saddened to hear of her demise. She seemed a pleasant lady.'

'And so her fiancé was Parnell de Vere?' Sergeant

Brown took out a pencil and began making notes but was stilled by a harsh look from his superior.

'And I understand that he will be meeting you the day after tomorrow?' LeGrand asked.

'This is correct,' the solicitor replied.

'Well then we will be in contact with you tomorrow.' LeGrand took to his feet.

'But it is Sunday tomorrow!' the solicitor bleated.

'Justice does not take the sabbath off, sir,' LeGrand countered. 'Speak nothing of this meeting, I tell you, or the full wrath of the law will come down upon you like a ton of bricks.'

Sunday was bright with the first real promise of Spring they had seen yet in the year. The hedgerows and the verges were full of new green shoots. LeGrand could see yellow and purple crocuses opening up under the morning sun. It pleased him. His heart was full and, although his mind was complicated, he felt, as he motored towards the house in Fobbing End, a touch of optimism in the fresh country air.

The Hearst house looked calm and restful, its eaves cosily wakening under the lemony rays.

As they parked their vehicle on the gravel drive, Constance came out to greet them.

She was alive and vibrant, blooming like the daffodils around her.

'Come in, come in,' she said to the men. 'Last night … and she put a finger to her lips. 'I have an idea.'

The offices of Grace and Sons were not dour, although there was an air of Dickensian neglect about them. The furniture was good and solid, yet groaned under the papers and binders that were piled up high. Mr Grace's view took in a rear garden. His rooms would have been bright if not for the large chestnut tree that was beginning to bud. Positioned on the first floor, with a westerly aspect, much of the light was blocked by branches.

'And so I should just proceed, as it were?' Mr Grace sat behind his desk and darted a glance at the door of the floor-length cupboard behind him.

'Yes, that's right,' LeGrand directed him. 'I think we can all agree, you will not miss our cue.'

Sergeant Brown broke in. 'And for goodness sake make yourself appear at ease, and don't, whatever you do, keep turning round.'

The solicitor brought his gaze back to them and fidgeted with his collar, attempting to loosen it. 'And I will not be in any present danger?'

LeGrand pointed to a partition wall set with a large window. It divided what had once been a spacious room into two separate offices. 'Sergeant Brown and myself will be just over there, and we have several constables downstairs and in the garden, primed to dash inside when we give them the signal. The crown jewels are not better guarded. You have my word, your safety is guaranteed.'

Mr Grace opened his mouth, but was stilled by the sound of a bell tinkling at the front door downstairs. 'That's him,' he said, and the inspector and his sergeant quickly made haste into the next room.

Although the window was hung with muslin and the interior lights put out, from their position the officers had a good view of Mr Grace's chambers.

LeGrand smiled. 'The trap is set.'

'And now for the fox,' his sergeant returned.

They stiffened at the sound of feet on the stairs, not heavy but weighty enough to convey the imminent arrival of a gentlemen.

Within seconds the door of Grace's chamber opened and in walked a young man.

Despite his similarity in height and build and his mane of dark hair, LeGrand could see at once this was not the same man he had interviewed on Saturday at Howlet Manor. There was a loose resemblance, it was true, but this newcomer was coarser by far. His comportment was strong and masculine, his hands rather more rough than a gentleman's might be. The fingernails were bitten down to the quick and, judging by the shudder about his shoulders, clearly he was in a state of some anxiety.

'Mr de Vere,' Grace sprang to his feet. 'Please take a seat.'

The imposter duly pulled out a chair and, doing his best to evidence a relaxed composure, seated himself.

'Refreshments?' enquired the solicitor.

The phoney declined. 'I do not have much time,' he said, his voice rough, full of unpolished consonants, and certainly not as refined as the genteel class he was trying to ape. LeGrand detected a quiver in the chap's lower vocal cords.

Gulping down some air 'Parnell' came straight to the point. 'The purpose of this visit is to make a request regarding the estate of my late fiancée.'

Mr Grace inclined his head. 'And once again, sir, I must convey my condolences.'

'Thank you. Then I would have you please make the cheque for Miss Hearst's immediate monies over to a friend of mine.' He sent Grace a sickly smile. 'I have of late, in grief, acquired some gambling debts. My friend will satisfy them when he receives the sum.'

Grace put on a pair of spectacles and drew out a pen, which fell clumsily on the desk. Without thinking he glanced at the partition window, nerves getting the better of him.

So intent was the charlatan on his actions, so full to the brim of his own dark purpose, that he did not ascertain the solicitor's tension.

Grace coughed, then asked, 'And who might this friend be, Mr de Vere?'

Bending over the desk the pretender whispered, 'It's Jack. Jack Boyd'.

At which point and with great drama, a low wail came up from somewhere in the room. It was preternatural, weary, of a strangulated texture that prickled the hairs on the back of the neck.

Both men froze.

Behind the lawyer the cupboard door sprang open, revealing there, in a position of great woe, a ghostly apparition in white. The face was hidden behind a flurry of gauzy veils and it wore a death shroud that, although it gleamed brightly, was gruesomely discoloured – shocking scarlet drips ran down from the neckline, gathering over the chest, and glinted wetly in the afternoon gloom.

The young man, Boyd, clamped a hand over his mouth as if to suppress a scream.

Mr Grace leapt out of his chair with a yelp and went to the window.

'Oh foul fiend,' began the watery voice of the spirit. 'Thou hast killed me.'

Floating forward, the wraith pointed a long white finger at the young man, no longer seated but now clutching his chest in a tremulous pose of shock and horror. The fellow's features contorted, his mouth grimaced and locked into an expression of black terror.

Halfway across, moaning in the most pitiful manner, the woman in white raised her veils. 'Recognise me?' she wailed.

The cowardly young man brought his hands to his face and hid. 'No,' he said. 'This cannot be. Constance, I did … you cannot have recovered …'

'You did what?' The apparition spoke with loud and strenuous condemnation. 'You sliced me in the churchyard and left me for dead, did you not?'

Now Boyd began to wail and, hugging his body with his arms, rocked back and forth in distraction.

Pressing on, the phantom persisted, standing over the cowering man, 'I cannot be at rest till the truth outs. "Doom'd for a certain term to walk the night.""

At which point Boyd, losing his wits entirely, cried out. 'I am sorry, Constance. I did kill thee. Though I wish it were not so ...'

Having now all the evidence they needed, LeGrand and his sergeant burst in from the adjoining room.

'Jack Boyd,' said LeGrand, taking the rogue by the neck. 'I am arresting you for the murder of Constance Hearst.'

As the felon collapsed in a heap on the floor, the true Constance Hearst took off her veils, revealing her vibrant brown locks. 'I told you it would work,' she said.

'And all of it took place in front of four of the most trustworthy witnesses of the parish: myself, a lady of fine reputation, albeit allegedly dead; one solicitor; and two intrepid officers of the law,' said Constance Hearst, whose undead status was very much in evidence. She did, indeed, just at that moment, seated round the table in the Fobbing House parlour, appear to be truly the most vivacious woman LeGrand had ever seen. He took a moment to appreciate the glow of her skin and the pink blush to her cheeks that may or may not have been enhanced by the application of Parisienne rouge.

It was a feast for the eyes, he thought. The events of the previous Monday had required much administration at the police station, and he had been deprived of Miss Hearst's company for six long days.

'You are to be congratulated on the success of your idea,' he said as she offered him a pretty plate of shortbreads. 'I must admit to having some misgivings ...'

Constance smiled and lifted a cup of tea to her lips. 'You must thank Mr Shakespeare for that, inspector. If I had not seen *Hamlet* the night before, it might never have come to me. But it worked. And now you have everything, correct?'

'Oh yes,' said the inspector. 'Mr Boyd was most anxious to get a confession off his chest.'

'Even though he had been told I was not a ghost?'

'The man seems to have been much troubled by his actions. Guilt preyed upon his mind.'

'Like Claudius,' Constance chimed in.

'Yes, I suppose so,' LeGrand agreed.

'So now, can you apprise me of the facts, as you promised? Then I will speak to the papers.'

And indeed LeGrand did.

It had, evidently, been Jack Boyd who had bumped into Bella, at the post office. Thinking her a fine lady he had been keen to offer assistance. According to the murderer he had actually introduced himself as Parnell de Vere's groom, which was indeed his position. But Bella, having already declared she was her mistress and perhaps full of both conflict and trepidation on the matter, had been too preoccupied and heard only the name Parnell de Vere. A mistake that Jack did nothing to counter.

After an enjoyable afternoon they agreed to meet the following week and a courtship grew up between the pretenders.

'It is very Shakespearian,' remarked Constance. 'A comedy of errors. Or a tragedy of such.'

'The items that she stole – a brooch, your cloak, the locket – were taken so that she might keep up the pretence of being you,' LeGrand said.

'Yes, I see that now.'

'It was not until her dismissal that events took a turn for the worse. While she was lodging in Haven, Boyd, sensing fragility, proposed marriage. Not long after the acceptance, at his urging, she agreed to draw up a will to bequeath him all her worldly goods.'

'Not that she had many, poor thing,' lamented Constance.

'But Boyd did not know that,' LeGrand spoke with soft insistence. 'He thought she was you.'

'And so what went wrong?'

'Well,' began LeGrand. 'We now understand that one afternoon, escorting his fiancée to her lodgings, they there ran into a delivery man on his rounds. Boyd was known to him and so he acknowledged his acquaintance. Of course, Jack feigned ignorance of the chap and promptly left. But we now know this delivery man warned Bella about the fellow, telling her to "be careful of that Jack. He's a no-gooder, and a ladies man". To which she replied, "You are mistaken on many accounts, sir. For a start that is Parnell de Vere." The delivery man had laughed loudly and immediately put her right. "That's not Parnell," he confirms in his statement, "but his groom, Jack."'

'I suppose Bella protested, did she?'

'She did but the man was insistent, "If he be Jack not Parnell then, mark my words, you'll find him in the Seven Stars tonight. Most commonly is." He then also left and, being in the Stars later himself, happened to make much of this incident to Jack and a group of his friends with a view to amusement and haranguing the groom. He had no idea that Jack would leave the inn full of temper to seek out his fiancée. The churchyard being on a rise and with a good view of the Stars, it did not take him long to find Bella, put an end to her investigation and start himself on the journey towards her inheritance.'

'Oh dear,' began Constance. 'It is a terrible shame. What a tangled web we weave ...'

'Yes, deception,' the inspector said. He met the lady's eyes, and feeling his own unenhanced blush begin to start, coughed and moved on to finish his tale. 'Boyd could not, of course, claim the will until Bella's body had been found. However, once the discovery came to pass, he was able to set his plan into action. The rest, I think, you can put together yourself.'

'Tragic,' Constance sighed. 'Poverty is the mother of crime.'

'But he was not poor, my dear. Jack Boyd had a good position as groom to Parnell de Vere that many would envy.'

'I was not thinking of him,' she said. 'Our cook has confided that poor Bella sent wages home for the keep of her siblings. Their father had died. I will wire them something when I have a moment. Bella was only trying to better herself.'

'That shows great compassion, Constance,' remarked the inspector.

And a silence settled on them.

'So,' Constance said at length. 'I find myself

doubly upset about this. For Bella and the trouble this caused her and for …'

But LeGrand cut her off, intent on demonstrating his own great depths of sympathy. 'Ah yes, indeed,' he said, thinking upon the end of the maid. It had not been pleasant. He would not wish a slow, freezing death in a cemetery upon his worst enemies.

'I didn't finish,' said Constance, and LeGrand felt ashamed. 'I am sad too that this has come to an end. Although it has been in many ways distressing – Bella, her family, the Boyd man – I must add, and I don't know if this is unseemly, it has also been rather exciting.'

LeGrand sighed. 'My life is never without excitement.' He was thinking of the paperwork and fresh cases he must begin on the morrow.

But Constance picked up his words. 'And is your wife's? Not without excitement? I mean, if you have a wife, then I doubt her life is particularly full of the ordinary. Not with you for a husband, surely? You do have a wife, no?' Her hand moved to the centre of the table. She smiled, almost coquettishly.

Emboldened by her approach LeGrand found himself delivering an uncharacteristic chuckle. 'Not yet,' he said and took her fingers in his.

And thus, it was fair to say that, The Harrowing of Constance Hearst did, in some way, come to an end. And something else, something quite unlike harrowing did also, in earnest, begin. For a few months, anyway.

CHRISTMAS DATES

Oh women – a constant source of joy and amusement.

The thought keeps me whistling even as the train chugs eastwards, the landscape opening to the sea. The sky is blue, the sun is low but bright. It's one of those brilliant winter days between Christmas and the New Year that come along once in a blue moon. The quality of light reminds me of some time I spent in the Alps, eons ago, on a school trip. So much has changed since then. I am a completely different person.

The world has altered too.

There are a few passengers in this carriage. Maybe five or six. More than I expected. We might be in lockdown, forbidden to make all but essential trips, yet people are tiring of being confined to their homes. People are bored. People are lonely.

Loneliness makes you take risks.

I am never alone.

Or lonely.

My head is full of optimism.

Each day brings with it the promise of new adventure, another scent, a fresh – or maybe not so fresh – delight.

I used to be a sad man.

Frustrated.

Some would say timid. Unpopular with the girls.

Until I met John.

John told me about bootcamp. It had transformed his life.

Once he shared his stories with me I immediately signed up.

Everything worked. All the hints and tricks.

I cast off the sad man and became … me. Bold, confident, adventurous.

Born again.

New.

I make my own way, follow my own rules.

Which is why I feel it's acceptable to flout the government's.

Screw them. They're meant for sheep.

I, however, am more of a lone wolf. Hairy, it's true, but some women like that. I keep myself trim and neat, mostly. Tidy up for dates. There's a few greys in my rather luxurious mane but I'm lucky that they're a deep grey. No white yet. Not me.

I catch my reflection in the window and emit a little groan of appreciation. Nice. Yeah, I'm ready for this.

The woman sitting a couple of seats down the aisle looks over and I realise I must have growled aloud. I try to send her a smile, then remember the mask will obscure it. I've a good mind to take it off, but there's a two-hundred-pound fine if they catch me. No one's worth that.

Instead, I turn away and look out of the window.

The masks work on a few different levels, I think. I'm happy to lurk behind mine. It provides a certain amount of protection, not only from the virus, but from showing your hand. It's all a game, you see, a charade. Not like those you play out of boredom with the family after Christmas lunch. No, mine is far more refined. Exquisite. Like chess – a strategy of moves and manoeuvres – illicit, sexy and scintillatingly dangerous liaisons. Entertainment unsuitable for those of a sensitive disposition. And I am a man who likes his thrills.

It's a fine day today.

Far too nice to spend inside.

Some time by the seaside will be just the thing.

And I will have *her*.

Theresa.

Hope she's worth the effort.

It's been over a month of chat. First on the dating app. Then the exchange of numbers. Messages. Daily. Reeling her in. Not that it was hard. This particular fish was not reluctant to come. At times I felt that she swam to me freely. Too quickly perhaps. The easiness of the catch I find disappointing sometimes. Everyone likes a bit of a challenge.

Sport has always been a big thing in my life, you see. Competition, which scared me before bootcamp, now delights. I like to win. I often do. And there are forums where you can post up your scores.

I'm quite legendary on some.

But Theresa was keen. Willing to meet, despite the pandemic and the caution and fear it has blown in with it.

Fresh out of a relationship that cracked this year, she lives alone. A Scorpio, apparently. Thirty-four. Never married. Brunette. Curves and a winning smile. A little on the short side for my liking, but like I said, the sea air will be a treat. And there's some who'd pay handsomely for a little tour of the town with an attractive girl on their arm. Especially now, when we're all going crazy with lockdown.

She's a looker, I think. In non-Covid times she could probably clean up, but all this social distancing has worked well for some of us on the dating apps. I've managed to score some quality. Theresa being one. Of course, the girls get attached. But, like I said I'm a loner, you can't pin me down. Once they like me, I tend to go off them. Can't help it. No challenge, and that's not my bag. And so I am forced to become a ghost. That is, I disappear. Without any further messages or calls. It's self-preservation really. Although there is something exquisitely tasty about another's discomfort that raises the spirits so. It is, I'm afraid to say, empowering to know that you are wanted, and yet strong enough not to want in return.

Perhaps it is weak to admit that, but, quite frankly my dear, I don't give a damn.

It works for me.

Every question mark message sent my way curls the shaggy hair on my loveable head. I must confess to taking screen shots of these texts as keepsakes to pass on. Souvenirs of my trips to different places, new towns, old villages, coffee shops, bars.

Each girl this year has her own image posted on

the noticeboard in the flat. There are fifty-one in all. Individual testimonies.

I intend to have one for each week by New Year's Eve. Theresa will be my last – number Fifty-Two.

Should have taken a shot of their pinned-up faces, smiling at me from their position on my bedroom wall. Some wistful, others bright, a few coy and pouty, holding their tummies in and taking sideways shots in dirty mirrors.

The thought of my conquests gives me a bit of a buzz, an energy boost.

Not that I really need one. I'm primed for the meeting. Pheromones are already zipping round my body.

A familiar tingle begins in my groin.

Of course, I don't in any way view these women as symbols of vengeance, you understand. It would be too easy to work the cod psychology and categorise me as a high-school loser snubbed by girls on that trip to the Alps, but now grown up and taking revenge. I'm way better than that. I put my feelings aside. What I do is skilled.

The train is slowing. It's my stop. Not that I've been here before. Looks all right though. Nice green hill on one side of the tracks, on the other a view of the sea with little boats bobbing up and down. The water shimmers. The tide is going out. There are a couple of clouds on the horizon now. Grey ones. I don't mind. I have brought my prop: a brolley. If the heavens open and the girl gets wet you share your umbrella with them. Cue big, wide-lipped smiles. They've seen it in the movies – then suddenly it's happening to them. Babes absolutely love it.

Even the feminists.

Suckers.

Now we've come fully to a halt, I disembark and pass through the barriers onto the concourse.

Theresa is there waiting, her body tight. I see her before she spots me and notice that her forehead is contracted. She looks stressed. First-date nerves. It's a good sign.

Her hair, curly not fuzzy as I imagined, spills out from under the red hood of her coat. She keeps patting it down, though it's a pointless task. It's untamed and wild. Needs a decent cut. I expect she's one of the sheep, who was too scared to go to the hairdressers when they said it was okay. Some people are so weak. And she's taller than she looked in her pictures. I like that. It'll make it easier to get going. There's only three days left of 2020 and I'm determined to get fifty-two. It's a goal. I have followers betting on whether I'll do it, desperate to see some of the texts the girls send. I've promised full disclosure if I make my target.

Theresa will be perfect.

Our eyes meet.

'Hi,' she says. Good cheekbones. Nice brows. Red lipstick to match her coat, though I think maybe I spy a slight strip of sweat that glistens on her upper lip. She wants to touch it but won't betray her nervousness publicly: her hand twitches but stays by her side.

I whip off my mask and make sure that she notices my wide smile before I look at the floor in a gesture of awkwardness, then make as if it's hard for me to meet her eyes. They love a dab of shyness. Brings out the maternal instinct, makes them try to overcompensate, shifts the balance of power. Not that they're aware.

'Hi,' I say back and make sure my cheeks dimple. 'You look great.'

And actually, she does. She has a long felt coat on, almost cloak-like. Christmassy. She's matched it with mustard-coloured gloves and red boots that have got a nice bit of heel. In fact, I'd say she was hot, and I'm not talking about her body temperature, though the thought of experiencing that broadens my grin.

Theresa's eyes twinkle. 'So do you,' she says and then sticks her twitchy hand towards a side exit and asks, 'fancy a walk by the shore?' She shakes her head at herself and titters. 'Sorry. That's all we can do – walk – isn't it? Silly me.'

I put my hand on her arm, noting she doesn't pull away, and say, 'Hey, it's okay. That would be lovely. I've just come to see you. Wherever you want to go is completely fine by me.'

I notice her swallow. For a second something dark, like doubt – probably self-doubt – flickers across her face, but she controls it and leads me out of the station and down a flight of steps, along a path bordered by fishermen's shacks.

All the time she is talking about the town: how old it is, the industry here, the characters and the sorts of things they get up to. And really I just want to tell her to shut up, but that wouldn't get me very far, would it? So I nod and chortle and make approving remarks.

The track opens out into a street full of pubs and cafes. Most of them are shut of course, but there's a booth that sells hot drinks where she stops and asks me if I fancy a coffee.

I start to say, 'Well, actually what I fancy, or more like "who" ...' and let that hang in the air.

She giggles. I quite like the sound. It's high pitched and full of energy, I might even go so far as to say loaded with tension. Sexual, I reckon.

Theresa makes a face and says something like, 'Oh you saucy devil,' but the words get caught up in her mouth and she has to repeat it, by which time it's lost its flavour and falls flat on the floor.

Gallantly I save her, 'Let me get them. I'm parched. A coffee would be great.' To be honest, I'd like something a bit stronger. Not because I want to take the edge off, but because I want to savour the moment, enjoy this time: I am absolutely killing it here.

I pay the girl at the booth and give her a wink. She doesn't smile back. Surly cow. She's got a mask on but you can still tell the expression underneath is like stone – there's an absence of creases around her eyes. This one just stares at me, gormless. Lesbian probably.

We fetch the drinks and sugar them, then wander along to the beach where Theresa suggests we sit down.

There's a bench with a good view of the water. We position ourselves about a metre apart and I start to ask her about herself. Stuff that hasn't come up before in our digital exchanges, like how long she's lived here and where she was before. It's good to get them talking about themselves.

Theresa, however, doesn't take the bait. Instead, the conversation turns back on me and how many dates I've had.

It's always hard to gauge the kind of answer a girl wants to hear. You don't want to look like you're not desirable. Likewise, it's all too easy to come across as a slag. I tell her five, which I think is acceptable for a pandemic, though a gross underestimate, of course. But she's good at this, and before I know it, we're having a conversation about me and what I want.

That's not right. I pull back and ask about *her* dates.

This is where she goes vague. 'Oh I went off it a bit, after I got ghosted,' she says with a self-deprecative shrug.

The word alerts me – ghosted. That's my realm. I inspect her with more care, but there's no way she's ended up on my corkboard. I'd notice, I think, but wish I'd got a photo of all the mugs up there, just to be sure.

'So nothing's worked out?' she asks, and then sends me a demure smile. 'Well, not so far …?'

Despite myself, I find the flirtation inviting. She's fit and they usually don't come on strong so quickly.

I like her style and so say, 'No. But I'm glad, or else I wouldn't be here.'

I wait to see how that goes down. Her reaction is promising: the shoulders relax and she turns into the sun and throws her head back. For a moment she looks incredibly attractive, like literally, and I chance it and slide my arm along the bench so my fingers touch her shoulder.

She gives out a small sigh.

An excellent sign, though not completely surprising. Everyone craves this.

The forced separation from each other, the lack of contact, the melancholic isolation have sensitised us to the merest of sensations – the waft of a butterfly wing, the ruffle of wind in the hair. Human to human physical interaction has become a rare pleasure. Indeed, it has replaced so many things, it's become our real treasure.

Still, though she's noticed my touch, there's nothing more, no further encouragement …

Interesting. Maybe she's not the sure-fire prospect I had her down as. No problem there. I up my game and am about to move my body along the bench when she pre-empts me and turns and stares into my face and says, 'You know, you have such incredible eyes.'

This wrongfoots me and I discover I am uncharacteristically pleased. 'Why thank you.'

Then she says, 'Windows of the soul, aren't they?'

A fitting phrase has floated to me – playful, flirty, a little bit dirty. Just right. 'All the better to see you with,' I tell her.

And she surprises me and claps her hands and says, 'Oh my god – you're perfect! I wasn't sure in our chats if …' then she catches herself, realising she's given too much away. It's best to play it cool on a first date. We all know that.

But I don't want her withdrawn and frigid, so I say, 'Do come closer so I can see you better, my dear.'

And she laughs and moves in, and we have our first little cuddle.

Neither of us say anything. The moment lasts for maybe a minute, then she draws away.

I don't want her to.

'Looks like rain,' I say and nod towards the growing bank of clouds about to cover the sun. 'Is there somewhere we can shelter?' Cheeky wink.

It's a gamble, but she finishes her coffee and crushes the cup. 'Good idea.' Then she's up. 'There's an island up here. Some beach huts on it.'

I thought she might invite me back to her place but she's obviously more cautious. Though the beach huts could be a contender for what I have in mind.

I follow her up to a sandy path.

Just before she steps onto it she pauses, turns to me and holds out her hand.

Result!

See – the merest of touches and we are charged.

This is the new world.

It won't be difficult to escalate this sexually.

I grab her glove and pull her into me. She doesn't resist and slips her other hand around my waist. I do the same and together we walk like this down the path, across a small bridge that runs over a creek, onto a low marshy island.

Day-trippers and dogwalkers pass us, going in the other direction, hurrying to get home before the clouds burst. Excellent. With no one around there's a lot we can do under cover of the bushes.

Theresa is becoming more responsive as we walk. She takes off a glove and lets her fingers slip over the hook of my belt, touching the soft flesh of my hip. I move my hand over her fleshy buttocks. Despite the cloak I can feel them tremble as she strides through the shrubland and find myself harden.

'Up here,' she says, and pushes aside a heavy branch.

There's a narrow track, though it is overgrown. We have to hold back foliage as we make our way through it. She's taking me somewhere secluded. I like it.

After five minutes we come out onto a small bank looking out to sea. It is surrounded by trees and quite private.

I feel a spot of rain on my cheek as she pulls me to the ground and finds my mouth. It is all quite sudden and I find it arousing. She's more than I bargained for. Perhaps I'll linger a little longer on this one.

Soon we are locked into a tight embrace, clothes sliding apart, delicious skin on desperate skin. I find my way into her and we buck and grind as the rain falls, spattering around us heavily until, sated, we fall apart.

She gasps.

It's a rewarding sound but all I can think is, 'Number fifty-two.'

Mission (and position) accomplished, I stretch out and yawn.

She's already on her feet, pulling up her jeans. Nice legs.

Her face is furrowed.

Sometimes they're like that when the lust has abated and they realise what they've done.

'Going so soon?' I say with a smile, not bothering to move. I'll lie here and let her appreciate the goods.

She puts on her coat and thrusts her hands into the pockets. 'I shouldn't have done that.'

'Why not?' I say. 'We're both consenting adults.'

'Look,' she says and shakes her head. 'It's not what I wanted. I didn't plan it like this.'

'Who cares? I like you,' I tell her and send her one of my soulful gazes.

She looks away. 'Don't worry,' she says and grins. 'It's not you. It's me.'

'Ha!' I say to her. 'The oldies are always the best.' I sound more cheery than I feel.

She starts again. 'I have problems doing this.'

What a shame, I think, now fast becoming flaccid. I misjudged her. She's just like the rest.

But then she's back. Kneeling down by my side, she bends over me, 'I keep being ghosted.'

'Damn,' I say, as if I'm being ironic. 'I thought I'd be your first.'

She moves her face to mine as if she's going to kiss me. 'My, what big teeth you have.' Then the bitch bites me.

I try to push her away, but she's snaked her arm underneath my shoulders and holds me close.

It's taken me by surprise, but I've got to say I'm not averse to a bit of rough and tumble. I like to think I'm pretty much up for anything.

'You're going to be my first,' she whispers.

Well, that's an enticing thought, so I relax and let her come in close again.

But as our lips touch, I feel something hard, metallic, thin, sharp, slice into my chest, knocking something internal, spearing off a shard of my rib.

Blood sprays over her.

My fingers try to reach for her cheek, but she lifts her face – full of triumph – and stabs me again.

Around us the light is beginning to fade.

A rumble of thunder begins in the distance.

The very last words, I hear, she whispers into me: 'I just thought it time I made a ghost of my own.'

Sod you, I think. This isn't at all how I saw this date going.

But all I can say is, 'Eat me.'

JOURNEY OF THE MAGI

A Triptych

I

FIRST MAGUS: THE FRIEND

The view opened up onto a marshy creek. A sea mist had sent its fingers into the potholes and crannies that dotted the banks on either side.

It was a marked change from Southend seafront where they had been only fifteen minutes before. The dirty neon lights that blinked in amusement arcades they had driven past made Maggie feel quite dismal. Although, to be fair, it wasn't necessarily the lights, but the handful of shady figures they illuminated: bent over slot machines and one-armed bandits.

Why would you be there, Maggie wondered? On Christmas Eve?

The thought was a conduction rod, and channelled a feeling that was not unfamiliar to her – a fusion of alienation, pity and 'unbelonging' which she had never found a name for.

The weather didn't help, she supposed. Rain had been coming down in sheets, lashing the taxi as it trundled through the drab vista. She had switched her eyes to the estuary for consolation, but found it sullen and bucking under fast-approaching thunderheads.

Presently, the coastal road retreated inland, and the landscape transformed. Instead of big chunky houses that glowered at the estuary, sixties developments jostled for prime position along the bends and curves of the road.

Away from the suburbs, vast flats of countryside stretched out for miles, unbroken but for small, stumpy hillocks and molehills. There was something wild and feral in the land that was both disconcerting and strangely enlivening.

What was it, she wondered, about this little group of islands that had so caught her friends, Hattie and Luke? She had believed them to be committed Londoners, thorough urbanites, yet they showed no signs of giving up their new-found country life and moving back to the smoke. Inevitably, she was keen to see just what it was that had sucked them away from her. She hadn't heard about the Essex archipelago, much less Sutton Island, on which they lived.

But her cabbie had.

'Many stories about this place,' he told Maggie as they turned left then right towards the North Sea and her island destination. 'No way I'd live here. Too remote. Too rural. Not enough life. Wouldn't come out for Christmas Eve. Not down this way. Not if you paid me.'

'I am paying you,' Maggie remarked. 'And I'm visiting friends, so it's them I've come to see. Not the place.'

The driver shrugged and shut up, taking the gear down as they passed the sign that announced they were in Iders End and should reduce their speed. Maggie expected everyone would be happy to do that: the only way onto the island was a dodgy, single-lane bridge.

It wasn't robust and creaked worryingly under the weight of the car.

Clip clop clip clop over the rickety bridge, she thought. What was that from?

Ah yes, the Three Billy Goats Gruff.

They reached solid land and passed through clusters of pines.

'Blimey,' said Maggie. The village ahead was like something out of a Brothers' Grimm tale.

Farm buildings reared out of the mist. A mauve outline of a windmill rotated its sails like a three-armed troll squaring up to hurl a boulder, and then she thought again of the Billy Goats Gruff – the little one, the medium-sized one and the great one. They had worked together to defeat the troll under the bridge. He had been butted far, far away so they could live happily ever after. Though she'd always felt a bit sorry for him and thought it was just a matter of time before he was bound to come back.

Silly goats.

Her gaze wandered out of the window. They had entered a narrow street dotted with white weather-boarded cottages. A couple sprouted satellite dishes like metal boils.

'Told you,' said the driver, assuming her expression had been born out of dismay. 'Gives me the creeps.'

But she didn't entirely agree. Underneath the fog and general gloom she could see it was an old village. Pretty in its own way. Well maintained, though tiny and cut off from the mainland on its own little island. A couple of the cottages looked empty but most had their lights on and she could see Christmas trees twinkling within.

The road became cobbled and bumpy. A hotch-potch of houses had been joined together, and nestled underneath a sign, 'The Half Moon'. Barrels in the beer garden had been carved to provide rustic seating and though they weren't filled, there were flower boxes outside every window. That'd be nice come summer.

The cab drove along for a couple of minutes before doing a sharp right through large iron gates that opened up onto a curving private drive. As they coasted round to the entrance, her driver announced, 'Here you are. Marsh House.'

Older than she had imagined, her friends' new home was impressive. It must have been one of a handful of buildings that stood over two storeys and was freshly whitewashed. Even in the drizzle the house glowed.

As they parked, there was movement in the portico and the front door flew open. Hattie, her good friend long missed, appeared in the doorway, her face split into a wide grin. She waved and bolted from the house before Maggie had swung her legs out of the car.

It must have been ages since they'd seen each other. Her friend's hair now curled and twisted past her shoulders into a shaggy lion's mane. Without her customary foundation Maggie could even see a smattering of freckles.

'Mags!' Hattie hugged her and shouted into her ear, far, far too loudly. 'At last. Did you have a smooth journey?'

Extricating herself from the clinch, she assured Hattie, still bouncing around like an enthusiastic puppy, that she had a good trip.

A cough from the taxi reminded her she had yet to pay the driver.

'Stay safe,' he said, and revved up and out of there.

'Now this is something else,' Maggie said, turning to survey the house. It was Georgian with large windows either side of the portico. She could see lights inside and jaunty baubles shining. 'God, you and Luke are so lucky.'

'Tell me about it.' Hattie picked up a suitcase and headed for the big oak door. 'Does not go unappreciated, I promise. Sometimes I wake up and still can't believe we live here.'

Maggie eyed the large glass lantern in the porch. Looked antique. Victorian she decided. There were lots of old bits and pieces around the place. The door knocker was fashioned in the shape of a woman's hand with three fingers pointing to the floor. Unusual. But she said, 'Beautiful.'

'Isn't it just? Eats up money like you wouldn't believe. Let me warn you: we've managed to get the outside sorted. Inside's another story. Been going through it room by room. The renovation budget's disappearing faster than you can say "Bugger off back to London."' Her friend turned on her heel and took Maggie into a large hall. 'I'll call Luke in from the back. He's chopping wood, if you can believe that! Lot of pigs flying around since we moved down here ...'

They had definitely changed, Maggie thought, as they sat round the kitchen table. Their transference to rural Essex had fleshed them out a bit. There was a breeziness in the way they spoke. Like they weren't in a hurry to be anywhere. Living in a place like this, Maggie didn't blame them.

Hattie was charged and full of energy. Luke, her husband, an IT consultant who perpetually worked late in various London companies, had lost much of his pasty office pallor. His face was fuller, and the tension that used to gather around his shoulders and crank them up to his ears had all but disappeared.

'With no mortgage to worry about, I've been able to take my foot off the accelerator a bit,' he told Maggie. 'And I've given in to Hattie and got a manager for the business.'

'At last,' Hattie said.

'Basically, so she fills up my day with jobs to do on the house instead ...' and his quick eyes twinkled with characteristic good humour.

'This is correct,' said Hattie. 'But look at it. Wouldn't you, Maggie?'

Yes, she thought, she probably would. If she ever happened to inherit a bloody massive stately-home-type crib, completely out of the blue, and had a husband who was both clever and practical and available and besotted. Sadly, neither were on the horizon, so she shut up and tried not to feel jealous. Hattie was her friend. She was pleased for her. Almost.

'So, do you want to then?' Luke finished his coffee. 'Look at it, that is?'

'Oh yeah,' said Maggie. 'I'd love to.' Why not? Hattie had said both the house and village were full of surprises, quaint customs, quirky architecture, colourful local characters. Sounded like an interesting little nook of the world, and she was always up for learning about anything new.

'Well, I'll take your bags up to your room.' Luke went to pick up her pull-along. 'I want to give Pete a call. You up for a quick one at the local tonight?'

'Oh yes,' said Maggie. 'Count me in.'

'They've got live music and there's a dance.'

'A dance? Um, not sure if I'm up for a disco …'

But Luke was already carrying her case to the stairs, calling over his shoulder. 'Hats, you show our guest the grounds while we've still got some light. Looks like it's stopped raining.'

'The grounds!' said Hattie and laughed. 'I still can't get used to saying that. Not coming from a flat where the only open space was a four-foot balcony.'

'Haven't even got a balcony,' muttered Maggie, but no one heard.

They rugged up and went out through a large wood-panelled living room, out through French windows on to a very wet and cracked but pleasant terrace.

'Wow,' Maggie remarked. 'An enormous garden.' It seemed to go on forever. An ornamental pond curled off to the left. On the right she could see neatly ploughed vegetable patches and greenhouses.

'You wait. The garden's the appetiser,' Hattie said as they marched over the lawn. Around the edges clustered thick and ancient oaks.

'Is that an orchard at the back?' Maggie could see that some of the trees were organised into rows.

'Yep,' said Hattie. 'It's unusually fertile ground here.' She coughed dramatically. 'Ahem, when the Ice-Age glaciers finished their gradual descent, they stopped around here in Essex, flattened it and then, as they thawed, deposited the debris that they'd collected on the way down. So we've got all sorts of soil.'

'That's right,' said Maggie. 'Essex has a complex geological structure.'

'Here we go,' said Hattie and rolled her eyes. 'Of course you'd know that.'

'The mix means it's arable,' Maggie said. 'You can grow most things in the Essex soil.' Her memory was remarked upon by all her friends. She thought it purely sponge-like, but not many others appeared to share the same factual recall. Hattie had told her to do more with it, but so far the skill had just made her a sought-after team player for pub quizzes.

'That's true,' said Hattie. 'But we're also fringed with waterways.'

'Over three hundred and fifty miles of coastline in the county,' Maggie said quietly and let Hattie continue waxing over her new home.

'So we've got samphire, mussels, oysters, and lots and lots of fish. Though, personally I don't really like to eat a lot of it. There's an MOD island next door and you don't know what they're putting in the water.'

'Oh,' said Maggie. 'Is that the main course to the appetiser? The weird island?'

'No,' said Hattie. They were coming out of the orchard now into a clearing. And as she said the words, Maggie saw it. 'We've got our own church. Well, chapel really.'

'Kidding me,' she muttered quite pointlessly. Because there it was, in front of her.

Although quite battered, four stubborn walls remained upright. Once upon a time the grand Gothic arches must have held stained glass. Now only their ossified outlines survived, blackened by what looked like soot. The decorative glass was long gone. The sloping roof, also black in places, was patched and broken. Up one end there was a tall steeple.

'Officially Our Lady of Miracles,' said Hattie.

'Not a unique name,' said Maggie. 'There's a couple of others in Italy, France … one in Goa I believe.'

Hattie ignored her. 'But the locals call it Our Lady's.'

Maggie surveyed the place. Ivy had eaten its way through the bricks and stones and rooted itself inside the crumbling keystone. It looked like the entrance could go at any minute, if it weren't for the two wooden posts that looked to have been recently erected to take some of the weight. She found it all a bit worrying.

'That's the bell tower.' Hattie pointed up.

Maggie could see at its top a chamber, with carved openings, that would have been big enough to house a large bell.

'Do you remember I told you about the Boxing Day parade?' Hattie nudged her.

'Oh yes, definitely. Sounds great. Brilliant.' She wasn't sure she had paid much attention to it when Hattie had told her about it on the phone. She'd been watching *Mastermind* at the same time.

'The villagers install a bell up there just for the day and ring it to call everyone in.'

Maggie nodded. 'Er, that's nice,' she said. 'Just remind me about the parade.'

'They come down the main street, up the lane at the side, through the garden and into the church. Then there's a small service. They call it Lady's Day. Sort of like Mother's Day. Every lady gets a flower.'

'But that's in March?' she said, then whispered. 'The fourth Sunday in Lent.'

'Bernard told me this one was originally called Modranicht – Mother's Night – and was on Christmas Eve. Celebration of Mary, Our Lady.'

'Well, that I don't mind. She went through an awful lot when she squeezed out the messiah. It's always about the baby, but think of giving birth in a blimmin' barn, surrounded by cows. Not the most sanitary of conditions. Good for her, getting a bit of adulation. But it's on Boxing Day?'

'Yeah, no one knows why they ended up celebrating it after Christmas. They do everything differently here. Suit themselves, really. It's so remote they can do what they like. But they love a bit of a rave-up. This is just a tradition though. It won't take long and we don't have to put much effort in. Pete said some people dress up for the parade, but we don't have to bother.'

'Who is this Pete, then?' asked Maggie, wondering if this was a potential set-up.

Hattie started moving across the grass which was littered with large stones. 'A friend we've made down here. You'll meet him later. He's nice. Single.'

'Really?' said Maggie and rolled her eyes. 'Quelle surprise.'

'You never know, you might like him.'

'Maybe. I'm not looking for anyone right now, but I'm open to offers.'

'I heard that, you loose woman.'

Maggie stepped across flat rock, then realised, to her dismay, it was a gravestone. 'Ew.'

But Hattie was already off again, 'We're not sure what to do about the place in the long term. The ground is uneven and some of it has caved in. Holes and crannies everywhere. Needs some attention. And structurally it's not really safe. But we can't pull it down. The locals would go nuts. And the bell tower is listed.'

Maggie was thinking about bells on Boxing Day. She was hoping to catch up on some sleep while she was staying. Work had been hectic this December. Even in the medical publishing business. They were always getting ready for spring and the new catalogue launch. So now she just wanted to relax and chill. 'Do we have to go to this parade? Is it early?'

'It's not till noon. Don't worry, you'll be able to have a lie-in and nurse your hangover.'

'Okay, cool.' She looked at the church. It was an odd thing to have at the bottom of the garden. Even odder to own it. She couldn't get her head round the idea, and wasn't sure if she'd like it if this was her property. 'Don't you don't mind the villagers using it? If it's yours?' Maggie slipped on the grass and righted herself, the effort forcing a grunt, which Hattie took for an expression of dismay.

'Oh, it's not that bad. They pop down and check on it. Leave flowers sometimes. But because they're so invested, they also help maintain it. Bernard from the pub's going to do some work on Boxing Day actually.'

'Weird,' said Maggie.

'Quaint. Historic,' said Hattie. 'Most families in the village have been here since *time immemorial*. They've got relatives in the graveyard. Only seems fair we should give them access. And can you imagine if us DFLs told them to keep off our land?'

'DFLs?'

'Down From Londons. Lots of us poncy media-types moving down Essex-way lately. Cheaper housing,' said Hattie. 'Plus me and Luke do want to settle here. We need to be accepted and you know how long that takes in rural parts.'

'You've got the family connection though. It's got to help,' Maggie said. 'Luke inherited the place off his uncle or something, didn't he? You're not complete *strangers*.'

'Yep,' Hattie nodded. 'Great Uncle Edward was well respected in the village. That does open some doors, but it's important to show commitment.'

'Oh yeah,' said Maggie. 'What was he like, the uncle?' she asked. 'Did Luke know him?'

'Edward Cecil Robinson-Devereaux. Sad really. Lived on his own. The neighbours think he wandered out into the creek, got caught by the current and that was the end of him. It's not unusual.'

'Really?'

'Yeah. Treacherous. You have to know every rip and tide.'

Maggie was starting to feel pleased she wasn't down here for long. 'And do you?'

'Well, we're learning. Actually, Uncle Edward wrote about it, which is handy. A notebook and a short biography that was put together as a letter.'

'Uh huh,' Maggie said and hoped Hattie wasn't going to suggest she look at it. So many people reckoned they had written a bestseller and wanted her to read it, with a view to publishing. She always stressed it was a *medical* publisher that she worked for, but people just tended to hear the second word and assume it was all the same. But she didn't work with fiction, she worked with fact. Though she was an avid reader of all genres. 'Epistolary,' she said vaguely.

'Eh piss what?'

'It's written like a letter.'

'Yeah, I started reading it,' Hattie went on. 'Quite interesting. Lots of pictures.'

'That's my level at the moment – books with pictures.' Maggie grinned.

'You should have a read,' said Hattie. 'It's on the coffee table in the living room.'

'Mmm,' said Maggie and sighed inwardly 'You get far?'

Hattie shook her head. 'No, I tell a lie ...' Hattie nodded to the church indicating they should start walking across the thick grass. 'I read the first few pages.'

Maggie followed. 'And?'

They hopped around sunken tombstones and ferns till they reached an old arched door.

'It's all right.'

'You're really selling it to me,' said Maggie.

'Yeah, but you never know. It might be a *bestseller*.'

'Okay.' Maggie sighed inwardly. 'Left my current book at home, anyway.'

'Deal!' said Hattie loudly. A huge flock of blackbirds took off from a nearby elm. She ducked and disappeared through the arch.

Maggie did the same, brushing ivy from her hair as she entered the church.

The floor was flagged with more cracked and ageing tombstones. Upturned wooden trunks scattered about were clearly used as improvised seats. At the sides a couple of long wooden pews leant against the uneven walls.

At the end of the church was a dusty platform with a large stone altar in its centre. It was quite roughly hewn, maybe medieval. Maybe older.

'Yeah, that's old,' said Hattie, watching her. 'But look, this is another reason why we can't knock this place down.' She beckoned Maggie over to a small slit in the far wall. 'Have a look.'

She squinted through it. Adjoining the chapel was a little room no bigger than a small garden shed. The far wall had fallen down, so she could see on to the graveyard on the other side, and the floor had collapsed into a dark crumbling grave-sized hole.

'Cool, huh?' said Hattie.

'Sorry, babe,' Maggie was unfazed. 'That doesn't look particularly impressive to me.'

'Not *now*,' said Hattie. 'But it was once an anchoress's cell.'

'A cell?'

'Yeah, you know. Like a monastery.'

'Was the anchoress a monk then?' She pushed away.

'Is this actually something you don't know?' Hattie gloated and went and sat on the altar.

Maggie thought it strangely disrespectful, but didn't volunteer her view.

'Back in the Middle Ages, when everyone reckoned crop failures and famine were the result of God's rage, to make sure of decent harvests, an anchoress would be given to the church.'

Maggie pulled up a pew. 'Given?'

'Yep. Some woman or girl would be selected from the community. They'd dedicate themselves to the church and live in that cell. It was meant to be an honour. Well, the family would get special favours after that.'

'Don't sound like a good deal to me.'

'They'd actually get walled up, interred. That narrow window was the only access they had to the outside world. It faced into the chapel so they could be given communion. They'd be fed through it too.'

'Say what?'

'Yeah I know.'

'There's a legend that the last one of them, Magda, fell in love with the priest who fed her. She helped them make poultices and medicines, was very wise. One day the priest smashed the walls of her cell and they ran away together. But fearing drought and ruin, the villagers found them and brought them back. On Lady's Day, however, the parish arrived for their service but the cell was empty, although perfectly intact. Both Magda and the priest had disappeared. Ascended to heaven. It was hailed as a blessed miracle, as, rather than fall into decline, using Magda's wisdom, the village prospered. She was the last anchoress. But she conferred grace upon the church.'

'Why isn't it called St Magda's then?'

'I think she's honoured on Lady's Day. Stands to reason doesn't it.'

'You don't know though?'

Hattie shrugged. 'It's not at the top of my list of priorities to be fair.'

She surveyed the cell again. Petite it was, bijou it wasn't. And certainly not her idea of a holiday home. 'You're keeping it, are you? Looks like a death trap, floor's falling through. Someone could do themselves an injury. I'm surprised the health and safety aspect hasn't freaked you out.'

'Oh, Bernard's going to come up and fill it in after the parade on Boxing Day. Flatten the floor so it's stable.'

'I don't like it,' said Maggie. 'You should get rid of it. It's sexist and creepy.'

'Can't. It's listed. No way.'

'Way.'

'There'd be uproar.'

'*I'd* get rid of it.'

'*You* don't have to live here.'

'*I'm* not sure that I'd want to.'

'There's an excellent local.'

'Fair enough,' Maggie said with a grin.

'Want to try it?'

'Absolutely,' said Maggie as they turned to leave. 'You can totally keep your church, the pub's my place of worship.'

'Amen to that,' said Hattie.

The Half Moon couldn't have been renovated for a good forty years: the walls were either exposed brick or white wattle and daub, flanked by dark wood beams, a nice garish inspiral carpet showed through to the grey underlay where it was threadbare. Slade's ever-present Christmas song played in the background, as quietly as it ever could.

The three friends got their drinks at the bar, then Hattie directed them to a table for four, which already had an occupant.

'You must be Pete,' Maggie said and shook his hand.

'Good to meet, at last,' he said. She saw his eyes appraise her for a moment longer than necessary. 'I've heard a lot about you.'

Luke slid in beside him. 'Pete's the community policeman,' he said.

He seemed pleasant enough, Maggie thought,

about the same age, not overweight, hair, no observable defects. She decided to make an effort. 'Do you live here, in Iders End?'

Hattie butted in. 'They call him a foreigner.'

'That is true,' said Pete. He had blue eyes and spiky black hair. Not a tall man, but he had something going on. 'I was born here but now I've got a cottage over the other side of the bridge so I'm technically an outsider.'

'But he's been good to us,' Luke patted him on the back. 'And we're bloody grateful. Showed us round, introduced us.'

'Ah, it's been my pleasure, mate,' said Pete with what seemed like genuine affection.

'What would we do without you?' said Hattie.

'Actually, you might have to for a while,' Pete returned. 'I've just booked a last-minute getaway for the twenty-seventh. Need a bit of winter sun.'

'Anywhere nice?' asked Luke.

Pete picked up his phone. 'Mexico …' and proceeded to show them photos of the resort, which they salivated over for quite some time.

After a while the landlord came over to collect the empties. 'Want a bag of mushrooms for the morrow?' he asked Hattie, which Maggie thought was another odd thing.

But then Hattie said, 'Oh yes please Bernard,' and introduced him. 'As well as running the most welcoming hostelry east of Brick Lane, Bernard's family also grows the best mushrooms in the land. You'll have to try them while you're down.'

'Oh yes, must have them while you're down,' he said to Beth. Then added to Hattie, 'I'll be up to sort that hole after the parade, all right?'

Luke, who had broken off from an argument about how to make the best margarita, butted in. 'You sure you want to do that, then? It can wait, or I can get to it in the new year.'

'It's no problem,' said Bernard. 'I've got all the tools anyway. Done it before, for your uncle. It's a regular hazard and I'm happy to help while I still can!' he chuckled. 'You'll be doing it soon enough when my arthritis finally wins.'

'Well,' said Hattie, 'come and have a drink with us afterwards, eh?'

'That'd be lovely,' he said. 'Mind if I bring the Mrs? I'm sure she'd like to see what you've done with the place.' He turned to Luke and Pete. 'You know what women are like with their interior decoration.'

Both men laughed.

Hattie, who did not seem put out by the gener-alisation but instead appeared pleased at the thought of showing off her half-finished home, said, 'Bring who you like, Bernard. Though remember it's a work in progress.'

'That's very kind of you, Hattie,' he said. 'We'll bring a bottle and another bag of 'shrooms.'

'Excellent,' said Luke and clapped his hands. 'Party!'

'Well, a gathering,' said Hattie and sent him a warning look.

'I'll be there with bells on,' said Bernard and winked.

Maggie fleetingly wondered if he was a morris dancer.

'Great,' said Luke again. 'You sure are a fun guy, Bernard. Funghi? Geddit?'

Everyone groaned. Bernard laughed the loudest, though he must have heard it a million times, and gathered up the empties.

Maggie swiftly finished her drink and offered to get a round in. She wanted to stretch her legs and look around.

She had a good vantage point, waiting at the bar. There was a small makeshift stage where a young man was setting up a mic and music stand. He sat down and settled a guitar on his knee then strummed a few chords, presumably the musical entertainment for the night. As Maggie watched him she realised the pub was probably the most happening nightspot in town. It was in fact the *only* nightspot in town. This was Iders End's version of a wild night out.

Centred in the middle of the room, hanging from the rafters, was a huge bunch of mistletoe tied together by a red satin ribbon. Holly and ivy had been draped across it with strings of pinecones and nuts. She had never seen such a big bunch of the stuff. It looked festive and entirely appropriate in the pub: traditional and pleasantly old-fashioned.

A roar of laughter went up from the public bar.

Maggie put her order in with an older woman, maybe Bernard's wife, just as a group of young people came in. Some of the louder girls wore flashing festive earrings and looked determined to capture the attention of an all-male group clustered close to the singer. The chatter increased in volume.

On the stage, the pub singer started up, introducing himself as Andy Mack – CDs available at the bar.

She took the drinks back to the table and popped them down around a brown paper bag that had been deposited in the middle. 'Those the prize mushrooms?'

'Uhuh,' said Hattie.

'You know what he grows them in?' Pete asked.

'Something I probably won't care to know?' Maggie replied.

Pete laughed.

'It's that old shed near the jetty, isn't it?' said Luke.

'But do you know what that used to be?' Pete looked like he was about to deliver a punchline. 'Ha ha,' he said. 'It was a morgue.'

'Bullshit,' said Luke. 'Doesn't look big enough to have been a morgue.'

Pete grinned. 'For a penny back in the day, Bernard's father, Abel, and his father before him, would "moor" the bodies of shipwrecked sailors there till they were identified or buried.'

'Vom,' said Hattie.

Maggie agreed.

Luke shook his head. 'He's having you on. Anyway, that wouldn't bother me. We've had them before. Tasty. We've had about five yields off him this year.'

Hattie nodded. 'Local produce.'

'Saturated with the souls of the dead,' Pete added with a wink. 'Seriously though Maggie, you should try them while you're down. They're big chestnut mushrooms, perfect for a Boxing Day fry-up.'

On stage the microphone crackled and Andy Mack announced he was having a short break, prompting the audience to surge to the bar.

Pete stood up. 'Let's go and get a good position.'

As they moved to the stage area Maggie watched a young man with a cropped haircut, who had been collecting glasses, nip over to the music system and surreptitiously slip on a CD. Instantly the pub was filled with booming bass and an MC bellowing out something incomprehensible. Bernard shouted over to turn it down, then called for Andy Mack to get back on again.

Climbing onto it with a loud sigh the musician picked up his guitar, but Maggie could tell he was faking his reluctance. He cranked up the amp.

Andy Mack went through a collection of the year's hits and some classic Christmas songs. The bloke could hold a tune, so they stood and tapped their feet.

Fifteen minutes later however, Hattie was yawning. Maggie leaned into her shoulder and asked her what time she was thinking of heading back. Luke, who had been jigging along to the last one, feigned indignation.

Pete also piped up. 'Oh come on. You've got to wait for Old End,' he said and winked at Maggie. 'It's a bit of a favourite here. Comes out on all occasions – weddings, funerals, bar mitzvahs and obvs Christmas Eve. Oh, hang on,' he looked back up to the stage. 'Talk of the Devil … Freddie's here.'

A shrunken old man in well-worn corduroys and a dusty military cap was climbing onto the stage. In his hands he held an accordion that looked far too heavy for his frail hands.

The young people, who had gathered at the front of the stage, immediately busied themselves pushing the remaining tables to the side and stacking the chairs against the walls.

The rest of the pub applauded as Andy Mack welcomed his guest, 'Frederick Wells – a legend in his own lunchtime.'

The old dude mumbled something nobody could hear, so Andy Mack moved the microphone stand closer to Frederick's mouth.

'Many a merry tune played upon an old fiddle,' Freddie rasped very loudly with a chuckle. Many people were by now quite inebriated and whooped loudly.

Other couples were moving down to the front excitedly.

This was clearly a participatory piece, Maggie thought, and took a step away, onto Pete's foot.

He winced theatrically then laughed, catching her elbow. 'Surprised you've cottoned on so early.' He bent his large frame to her ear. 'You seen it before?'

She shook her head. 'I'm guessing this is some kind of traditional, regional folk dance associated with fertility, virility, but often camouflaged with manners and gestures of social etiquette?'

'Almost. Just watch.'

Overhearing, Luke called over to Pete. 'Think our city slicker will be in for a surprise.'

'Fuck off,' said Maggie at the very moment everything grew quiet.

A couple of frowny faces turned her way, but most people were more focussed on the stage.

The accordionist began to play.

'Oh I am a gentleman of plenty,' sang Andy Mack.

'And I am a man alone.

But when I spy the girl I want

I'm a gentleman of none.'

And with that last line she saw him reach down behind his chair and produce some kind of large black spiky thing.

Shrieks of delight erupted from the centre of a dance floor that had appeared before the stage.

The singer waved what he was holding at the throng, then he tossed it up and into the crowd.

Hands went up in the air, people scrambled over each other in attempts to catch it.

The song bounced off into the first chorus and the rest of the pub closed in on the dance floor. Pete put his arm round Maggie's shoulders and gently propelled her forwards.

'No thanks,' she said. 'I'm more into spectator sports.'

'Come on,' he said, and nudged her forward again. 'You look like you could do with a bit of fun. Relax.'

Maggie glanced about for Hattie and Luke and saw they were already up front, clapping to the action on the dance floor.

Propelled on by Pete, she joined what was now an outer ring made up of the bar staff and the older punters. Inside that, the young crowd had formed – from what just moments before had been a scrum – an ordered inner circle. Boys had grabbed girls, girls had grabbed boys, and now, all hands linked in a chain, they set off at a pace, speedily, whirling round the centre, where a solitary lad jigged alone.

Ah, thought Maggie. Got it – he was the lad who had caught the prize Andy Mack had thrown out. She could see that because he'd strapped it on to his head.

Now he looked at least seven feet tall, his height enhanced by bony antlers that twisted from his skull.

It looked strange to her, but everyone else was loving it, clapping their hands and stamping their feet to the rhythm of the song.

As the pace increased, so did the speed of the inner-circle dance. The boy with the antlers groaned loudly and began to the scrape the ground with his feet, like a bull readying to charge. He laughed, snorted and then made a speedy dash at one of the female dancers but failed to grab her.

The inner ring shrieked with amusement; the outer circle tittered humorously.

Stag/boy made another attempt and another, then, as the music reached a crescendo, he galloped at a woman in her late thirties with a thatch of platinum hair. Managing to trap her in his arms, he brought his prey back into the centre and pulling down some of the overhanging mistletoe bunch kissed the blonde heartily and with obvious passion.

Feeling uncomfortable, Maggie darted a glance at some of the older customers expecting disapproval – there was none in their faces. Surprisingly it was quite the reverse – absolute approval.

The inner circle broke up and joined the outer. Those who had been on the edges grabbed a partner and began to move in a jagged, loping way, in a dance that resembled something halfway between a polka and a jive, as the fiddle kept up its raucous tempo.

Rowdy and noisy, soon she could only see a mass of faces and bodies jigging in a circle round and round the dance floor. She glimpsed Hattie and Luke somewhere over by the stage but then they were lost in the swirl.

'Come on,' said a voice next to her and she felt Pete's arms fasten round her waist. She hesitated for a moment then told herself 'Why not?' as she gave in to the flow and let Pete guide her off to the nearest section of the circle. It opened to receive them and then soon they too were whirling and spiralling in the dance.

It ended abruptly with an eruption of applause and shouts from the crowd.

People bowed to each other, panting.

She felt Pete release her so she took a step back and curtseyed like the other women were. He bowed too and offered his arm. Panting, they left the dance floor.

Pete dropped her back at their old table. Luke and Hattie were already there. The boys immediately resumed their chat.

'Oooher,' Maggie said plumping down beside Hattie. 'You come here often love?' Her friend's cheeks were flushed.

'They like a bit of a jig down here.'

'So I see,' Maggie laughed.

'Been doing it for years,' said Hattie. 'Pete reckons it's all "touristy play acting".'

Maggie looked around. 'Can't see no tourists here.'

'Well,' said Hattie. 'Not so much at Christmas. I mean, who wants to be marooned out here if the cab doesn't come.'

'Me!' said Maggie, realising that actually she was having some quality, if unusual, feel-good fun.

There was a loud clang of the bell and Bernard called time.

She was surprised there wasn't going to be a lock-in, as they were miles away from the local plods. But then she supposed it was Christmas for Bernard and his wife too. They, no doubt, would have just as many preparations to make as anyone.

The group finished their drinks and made for the door.

'Happy Christmas,' Bernard yelled over to them. 'See yous Boxing Day. I'll bring a bottle.'

Tired and exhausted, and quite tipsy, they ambled up the lane.

Maggie noticed it was remarkably quiet outside. So different to town.

In the distance they heard a couple of cars leaving the pub car park but up here, towards Marsh House, there was nothing but the crackle of dry bracken and the whispering of the wind in the treetops.

And it was getting blimmin' colder by the minute. A frost was coming down. Even the mice and voles had taken shelter underground.

Something screeched from the nearby tree.

They all jumped.

'What was that?' Maggie gasped as she caught hold of Hattie's arm.

Luke laughed and stamped his feet against the cold. 'It's a barn owl.'

'Oh,' said Hattie, and she and Maggie laughed.

There was a glint of wing feathers in the moonlight, and a white shape swooped silently across their path. Pale yet luminous, like the ghost of a baby flying over the garden, it arched over the house and settled on the roof and let out a scream.

This time Maggie did not laugh.

It sounds like a warning, she thought.

Christmas day came and went without much deviation from the usual routine.

They exchanged presents over breakfast, which was a light meal – they were all a bit queasy, so nobody objected. Hattie said she'd do a full fry-up on Boxing Day to line their stomachs, if they were having drinks straight after the parade.

And, as it was, it was a good call because Christmas lunch was served on the dot at 2 p.m. Coming with all the trimmings, it filled their stomachs beyond capacity. They flopped on sofas as they watched the Queen's speech on the television. Then it was more wine, charades, liqueurs, Trivial Pursuit, Irish coffee, and finally a James Bond movie during which Hattie and Luke dozed off.

Left to her own devices, Maggie looked around for a book or magazine to read. On the coffee table was a notebook, dog-eared and leather-bound, with the name Cecil Robinson-Deveraux inked across it. Her hands moved over the front and opened it. The action released the smell of dust and old books.

She turned to the front inside page where spidery words had been penned in a dark, navy ink.

'*To whom it may concern.*'

There was nothing else. She turned over the page.

You were probably expecting a journal. I myself was intending to write such a thing but, as has been pointed out, a diary suggests more permanence than a letter. The reader may be reticent to destroy a book, imagining it may have some worth to offer later generations, some gems to bestow.

This does, of course.

Maggie continued, fascinated. The paper beneath her fingertips felt fragile, like moth wings. As if one sharp movement or tug, and they might crumble into powder.

Nevertheless, it must be destroyed after you have read it.

So a letter this must be.

It would be true to say that at one point, indeed, I did consider a tome. If you could spy me now, you would see an old man shaking his head, appalled at his folly. The error of that has never been more evident. I cannot put the imprudence down to youthful optimism: I was sixty-five years old when I returned to Iders End. Old enough to know better.

A while later, Hattie snored and woke herself up. 'Oh hello,' she said. 'What time is it?'

Maggie couldn't lift her eyes from the page: *Interestingly the owl is associated with goddesses.*

'Gone ten,' she told her friend.

'Blimey. Shall we call it a night?'

And Maggie, whose eyes felt at once heavy-lidded, nodded. She returned the book to the table and bid her friends goodnight.

In her room, sated and half-sozzled, immediately she fell deeply asleep.

Boxing Day morning was low and overcast and not very Christmassy at all. But that didn't stop the residents of Marsh House doing their utmost to keep the festive spirit going: crackers were pulled at breakfast almost as soon as they sat down. Once the jokes had been read out, paper hats put on and cracker trinkets moaned over, Hattie made coffee.

Pushing down the plunger on a tall pot, she giggled. 'Fancy being naughty and having a nip of whisky in it?' she asked. 'It's almost still Christmas after all.'

This was a very good idea, they agreed.

The girls moved on to Buck's Fizz while Luke served up breakfast.

The sausages and bacon were apparently the work of 'Pete's friend, Keith', Luke said and winked at her. 'A retired policeman. He's a pig-farmer over in Barling. Do you know that pork tastes like human flesh? Allegedly.'

Hattie tutted. 'Luke!'

Her husband returned the sharp look with schoolboy bafflement. 'What?'

'You'll put Maggie off her breakfast.'

A dishcloth landed on Luke's head.

Luke looked at his plate of food. 'Right, well, we should scoff this as soon as we can. The parade will be on its way soon.' He looked at the clock on the wall. 'Three quarters of an hour. Can we do that?'

'Oh yeah,' said Maggie and began on her beans.

'Got to eat the mushrooms,' Luke urged. 'Or I'll tell Bernard.'

She laughed, but then seeing he was serious, cut one up and stuffed a piece in her mouth. It was juicy and meaty and hearty.

Surprised to discover she liked them, she wolfed the rest down quickly.

'The parade will be good,' Luke said. 'A bit of local custom. You're lucky that you're invited in. It's usually locals only.'

'I shall demonstrate my appreciation through an outward display of decorum,' Maggie said.

'Better late than never,' Luke beamed.

'Cheeky.'

'I'm looking forward to it,' he went on. 'I quite like a bit of hymn-singing.'

'Well, we should get on with it,' said Hattie. 'Go and put your glad rags on Mags.'

'Mmm – glad rags and wellies. That'll be a good look.'

The garden of Marsh House was teeming with activity. Villagers were streaming in from the lane, cutting up the side of the garden through the orchard and on towards the chapel, human features camouflaged by different masks.

'Bloody hell,' said Maggie. 'You didn't tell me they were dressing up like this.' She laughed and pointed to a stocky man in a lose coat wearing the head of a hare. On his arm he supported a tipsy blonde with the sly face of a fox.

'Shh,' said Hattie. 'They'll hear.'

'I can't help it,' said Maggie. 'I'm pissed.' And she realised she was.

Just behind them, more of the locals followed, sprouting antlers, ears, beaks. Some were singing and chanting. There was a faint jingling of bells. Above that the rhythmic beating of a drum.

'Come on,' said Hattie, as Luke caught up with them. 'We're the lord and lady. Got to show some leadership here.'

'True,' said Maggie but a sudden wave of

dizziness overcame her and she felt herself stagger to one side.

'You all right?' Luke asked.

Unwilling to admit she'd drunk too much she just nodded.

He pointed towards the chapel. 'Come on. Otherwise we won't get any seats.'

Up ahead a clutch of nubile figures appeared to be spinning round and round. The sight made her feel dizzy again so she concentrated on the people in front, though it wasn't comforting. They were reptilian in appearance, one wearing a frilled lizard's head, the other green and scaley like a snake. Both were rigid in striped clothes like pyjamas.

As they neared the chapel she heard voices raised in song. Too quick and frenzied for hymns.

Something behind them howled. Maggie spun round. A stream of shadowy figures were following.

'Come on,' urged Luke. 'Plenty of time to appreciate the costumes once we've got our places.'

He broke into a canter as they left the orchard and crossed the clearing.

Maggie sped up and followed them. By the arch was a little girl giving flowers to the women, strange poinsettia-type blooms with purple tendrils that swayed. Maggie wasn't bothered. She took one and put it in her hair, ducked through the arch and stumbled into the chapel.

It was already full.

The only seats available were right at the front.

As she walked down the aisle she noticed bright light spilling out of the tiny window in the anchoress's cell. Probably a bunch of candles, thought Maggie. Very bright ones.

Hattie knocked into her and nearly fell. Luke propped her up and manoeuvred her along the row full of makeshift benches, then sat her between himself and Maggie. Her head flopped forwards limply.

Maggie sat down. 'You all right?' She was feeling a bit odd too. Time seemed to be slowing.

'Fine,' said Hattie through half-closed eyes and sent back a dozy smile.

'Here,' said Luke and passed a hip flask over. 'A little Christmas present from Pete. Single malt.'

Maggie shook her head. Something in her tummy was starting to object.

'Go on,' Luke said.

Hattie added, 'It'll put hairs on your chest.'

'No,' Maggie pushed it away, a little more roughly than intended. 'I don't want it.'

'Your loss.' Luke shrugged and passed the

unstoppered pewter bottle to Hattie, who took a large swig and gave it back.

'Treacly,' she said and hicced.

Luke took another draft. 'Blimey, that's good.' He coughed as it caught in his throat. 'Strong though.'

From the bell tower a long, sustained peal rang out, loud enough to be heard all over the island.

As it faded a hush descended over the gathered congregation.

A thrill of excitement went through Maggie.

With great ceremony three masked men with antlered headdresses escorted a female priest on to the platform.

A female priest, thought Maggie. That was quite wrong. There was a name for them, wasn't there? Ah yes, priestess. But that also sounded weird. Here, in a church. And she wasn't dressed as an ordinary woman clergy-person.

This one stood in front of the altar and raised her arms, spectral and impressive in pristine white robes that seemed to shine.

Wow, thought Maggie. It was an effective piece of theatre. The air above the woman was glistening. Her head was garlanded in flowers. Maggie decided they glowed artificially bright. In fact, come to think of it, everything looked like it was being filmed in technicolour. Through the patches in the roof, the sky above appeared pink, alive with energy.

Maggie turned round and had a look behind her. The church was packed. The locals in their strange headdresses had now morphed into weird half-human hybrids. But at least they were smiling.

Smiling straight at her.

That's nice, she thought.

And actually she was completely fine about everything, although maybe a little flighty, giddy. It was a feeling that reminded her of festivals when she'd sampled illicit drugs.

And this, indeed, was some full-on trip, she thought, and, as she glanced around again, she couldn't help but giggle.

Hattie, who was sitting next to her, nudged Maggie and began chuckling too. Then Luke, who looked like he was doing his best to appear sober, said 'Shh.' There was a lisp to his words, his movements were slipping, a languor coming over him, eyes thick-lidded and fuzzy.

Maggie's stomach groaned. Blimey, she thought, we're all really, really pissed.

We shouldn't have gone as far as that second bottle of Buck's Fizz with breakfast. Not after the whisky.

Breakfast.

Oh yeah.

This wasn't good.

The thought of food was making her queasy.

And now the priestess was speaking, slow and deliberate. Maggie couldn't understand a word. She turned to Hattie, but was surprised to see she'd fallen asleep on Luke's shoulder. He too was struggling to stay awake.

Although Maggie felt drowsy, she wasn't as bad as them. But then she'd always had a strong stomach.

Still, her head wobbled unsteadily upon her neck. Trying hard to keep it straight she stared at the altar – something was going on. The priestess had something in her hand. A golden goblet. How glamorous.

The villagers were lining up the aisle, shifting along, as each person presented to the priestess was offered a sip of the cup. After they had drunk, they returned to their seat.

'Come on,' said a voice beside her.

She turned slowly to see a giant black crow at her shoulder. It seemed both odd but also simultaneously absolutely natural, absolutely normal. Given where they were.

The crow's head cocked to the right and then slid

up over a forehead and she recognised the face that had been hidden underneath.

'Pete!' she said. 'The commune ...' she laughed. What was the word? 'The commune's policeman?' Then she got it, though the words wouldn't come out properly. 'The commonitee policeman!'

'Yes,' he said and opened his arms.

''Ello, 'ello, 'ello,' said Maggie. 'What's all this going on 'ere then?' Then she laughed.

'Let's get you up,' he said and fastened his arms around her. 'Come and have communion.'

As he lifted her up, she was visited by the briefest of notions that maybe, perhaps, she might resist him, but she discovered then that she couldn't be bothered. Despite the growling in her tummy and her giddiness, she continued to feel completely fine. In fact, more than that; she was pleased to be here. She was having a great time.

And the big strong arms that propelled her up the aisle felt nice too. She was having a job to walk straight, so needed Pete beside her anyway.

The priestess smiled when she was presented. 'Ah,' she said. 'And here we are.' Holding the goblet to Maggie's lips, she urged her to drink. But this wasn't a golden goblet, it was a black one. With dark liquid within.

'Okay,' said Maggie and sipped.

'Have some more,' said the woman. Maggie wondered if perhaps she was the anchoress.

The wine was sweet – thick like syrup – and tasty, and so she gulped again.

Though it was going straight to her head and interfering with her limbs that were thick and heavy and getting slower and slower still, not doing what she meant them to.

Time *was* becoming sluggish, she thought now. Or was it going sideways?

It was a funny thing, she thought and held on to Pete as her legs buckled. 'Can't stand,' she said.

'That's okay. Let's get you up here for a lie-down.'

She could tell from his voice that underneath the crow's beak his lips were smiling. In fact they all were – the hare, the strange reptile and the woman with the flowers in her hair, the four birds – robin, blackbird, owl, eagle.

So nice of them to lay her down, here on this cool stone slab. So nice of them to spread her hair as the darkness did descend. So nice of them to hold her hand as the priestess loomed over her. So n—

The sound of the door slamming woke Hattie up.

God, her head ached.

What on earth had happened?

She could see evidence of a gathering, maybe a party, in the living room: champagne bottles and beer cans, party poppers, streamers and halves of pulled crackers were strewn all over the floor. Luke was out cold on the sofa opposite, still upright clutching a beer in his hand.

Outside the windows it was black. What time was it?

Someone bustled into the room. Hattie blinked as he approached. It was Pete. Thank god. Relief coursed through her. Though she wasn't exactly sure why.

'Right,' he said brightly. 'That's the last of them gone. Sorry about that. Some of them do tend to outstay their welcome. I think they were just nosey and wanted to see what you'd done to the place.'

Hattie rubbed her eyes. 'Who? What?'

Pete pulled over a pouffe and sat down near to Hattie. 'Don't you remember? Bernard filled in the floor as he promised, and then he and Lyria came back for drinks. And they brought a few friends as you'd told them it was open house. There was about twenty in here.'

She shook her head. 'Oh my god. I have no memory of any of this.'

'No,' Pete said. And then he grinned. 'The three of you were already rather spannered. You and Luke fell asleep when we got back. But it was the sort of do where no one minded. The drinks flowed freely and everyone seemed to have a good time. I think it went on a bit longer than some of the women would have liked. Now don't worry, you sit there, I'll clear this lot up.' He got up and went into the kitchen.

Hattie gazed around the room. There was something that wasn't quite right. At last she called out, 'Where's Maggie?'

Returning with a broom, Pete began sweeping up. 'She got freaked out and decided to go home.'

'What?' said Hattie.

'You had a bit of a fight. Or she and Luke did.'

'Really? What about?'

He pushed the detritus into a pile. 'Drinking whisky in the church, I think. Well, that's what Luke told me.'

Yes, she had some vague memory of that. 'Better phone her,' Hattie said and began to struggle up from the sofa.

'Oh I wouldn't,' Pete stopped her. 'She said she wanted some space.'

Hattie frowned. 'That doesn't sound like Maggie. You sure she was all right?'

'Yeah,' he said. 'I took her to the station. She'll be nearly home.'

'Well,' said Hattie, becoming more insistent. 'I'm going to call her anyway.'

But Pete lightly pushed her back. 'I seriously wouldn't bother. No reception on the Tube is there?'

Damn, thought Hattie, he's right.

'And by my reckoning,' Pete looked at his watch and leered. 'Right now – she'll be underground.'

II

SECOND MAGUS:
THE WISE MAN

Cecil Robinson-Devereaux

[Incomplete transcript]

To whom it may concern,

You were probably expecting a journal. I, myself, was intending to write such a thing but, as has been pointed out, a diary suggests more permanence than a letter. The reader may be reticent to destroy a book, imagining it may have some worth to offer later generations, some gems to bestow.

This does, of course.

Nevertheless, it must be destroyed after you have read it.

So a letter this must be.

It would be true to say that at one point, indeed, I did consider a book! If you could spy me now, you would see an old man shaking his head, appalled at his folly. The error of that has never been more evident. I cannot even put the imprudence down to youthful optimism: I was sixty-five years old when I returned to Iders End. Old enough to know better. Yet, for my part, I may say that I was always taken by the stark beauty of the landscape and the quaint rural customs, the distinctive native fauna and wildlife. They filled me with fascination and wonder. The rare qualities in this habitat of Iders End, were what drew me in to investigate further. And it was as I looked closer into the realm of nature that I began to wonder about certain phenomena – the pale creatures, the geological rarities, the XXXXXXXXXXXXXXXX.

[line redacted]

[pages missing]

[cont'd] *words I commit here pertain to that.*

Upon my return here (or was it my second visit? Third?). I was reacquainted with my home village that I had largely forgotten. Indeed, it seemed that Iders End was untouched by the passage of time (though how wrong could I be?). I imagined leaving a record of the place and customs would be a noble and worthy cause, to preserve the last vestiges of a different way of life lest the military took the land and no common fellow be admitted any more.

The notion of writing, of becoming a writer, attracted me. What better occupation for a recently retired civil servant who enjoyed roaming the land and, in addition to that, had a passion for the pleasures of the pen?

I speculated that an 'autumnal career' might provide an expressive outlook and also open doors into new circles. And for a while I fancied myself as a southern Wainwright, exploring the curve of South-East England, perhaps setting out several walks to enable the tourist to appreciate the beauty of our little corner of the globe. Indeed, I made a good start on several books – an illustrated tome that sought to capture the wildlife, a collection of family names and traditions, another illustrated volume that detailed fauna and flora and a potted history of agriculture.

These studies of course came to present such irregularities as things made themselves clearer. With a sharp gaze led by curiosity and a recall of my own personal history I soon began to see beyond the superficial. Thus, as the exceptional nature of what resides herein dawned on me, I realised my work was reckless, that I could not, would not, reveal any more.

But I digress.

Apologies.

At this point, I must tell you, you should know my intentions are good. They have always been so. In the past, I must admit, at times they have been misguided or lacking in the subtle comprehension required to understand Iders End. But I am correcting that now and shall destroy and obliterate where necessary. I commit to this paper only what may help you so that it may illuminate your path. It is the last thing to do before I set forth to follow my own.

Your forgiveness is required should you find pages be omitted. I am aware of the approach of Lady's Day, the sand dripping through the hourglass. Therefore my words appear as they flow out of my hand. There may not be time to rewrite to perfection. But, of course, you will not understand. Just appreciate this – I cannot be comprehensive and at points may appear oblique. This is not wanton, but simply cannot be helped: imparting such knowledge is like the dropping of a great stone into a small pond: it creates more than mere ripples, it changes the direction of things. We must be careful and take pains not to alarm you: it is necessary you remain to complete the cycle.

Things are for you, at present, confusing. Were it any consolation, I should tell you, I have been through the very same cloud of mystification. You will come out the other side, so know that now. And bear with me, your humble narrator – all will become clearer come Modranicht.

In truth it takes a lifetime to fully understand the nature of the place. A small dose of such knowledge *alone can unhinge frail minds. There are many here that would not cope so well, if it were not for the soporific effect of the Valerian mushrooms, a species that is unique to this area. Where nature takes, it gives also.*

Sutton Island is distinguished from the others by way of the village of Iders End. Not only is this settlement one of the oldest in the area, predating Saxon occupation, it supports a community largely reliant on farming the land, whose relationship with and respect for its inimitable qualities have not been washed away by the tides of time.

The inhabitants of Iders End exist in something of an awkward harmony with their neighbouring occupants of Foulness. For many years, the land has been occupied by the military. I often wonder why they came here? Perhaps for the same reason our ancestors did, drawn to the isolation, the difficulty of reach, the exclusion, the limp, seemingly uninteresting land that camouflages the magnetic and altogether unearthly properties that exist in this location.

Religion has always produced explanations for aspects of life we are unable to understand. And that is the same here. The miraculous is unexplainable and unique – exactly the reason it becomes holy. In Iders End, I believe these mysterious qualities, perhaps even anomalies, are acknowledged, rationalised and then disguised within the celebration of the divine presence – The Lady – whose origins may well reach far back into the beginnings of human provenance.

And yet I wonder also if her gateway was reawoken by my own mother.

But I will come to that soon enough.

Remember also the anchoress. The story of which I am sure you know now. She is of great significance. As you will discover.

Not long after my homecoming, I assumed that Our Lady was Mary, mother of God, another creatress. But as my studies moved along I began to wonder if she, as depicted in her form here, may be an embodiment of Nature. Mother Nature.

Although I had spent much of my time overseas, I had not been out of reach of new ideas and had heard much talk of Lovelock's theories concerning Gaia. His contention was that the planet we live on interacts with its surroundings to maintain its habitability. It certainly struck a chord with the zeitgeist of the time. And I wondered if, in naming his theory after Gaia, the Earth Goddess, he was alluding to this purpose in nature? It was a fashionable conceit then. Not so any more. Whether or not Lovelock ever intended a link to be made, in some circles Gaia was equated with Mother

Nature and Mother Earth. It struck me that Our Lady indeed might be the personification of these abstracts.

I now consider that doubtful: those names evoke an overriding sense of nurture and, as I was to find out, Our Iders End Lady, though benign, can exhibit a powerful belligerence, the likes of which I have only seen in comparable Asian deities, such as Kali. The Hindu goddess of death, time and change, a wild she-god, who devours her children. I recall, on a visit to India, viewing paintings of the deity that rendered me instantly cold. Like her sister in Albion, Kali too was womb and tomb. Life and birth are eternally bound to death and destruction. Like yin and yang, two sides of the coin. As with Kali, our goddess too can escort Death. And it would be untrue to say there is no blood spilled for her here. Though she gives life, she will also take.

But this understanding takes time. Until we can comprehend its true nature, that the old ways are revered and kept is of utmost importance. They guard and obfuscate the marvels herein. Because they are conceived as sacred they are, in essence, occult – accessible only to the privileged, the initiated. As our military neighbours appreciate – with secrecy comes protection. Of course, a filtered copy, a carbon facsimile is presented on occasion to please onlookers when curiosity becomes too keen. But it is nowhere near the strength of the real, which must be hidden to the outside world, at all costs.

This is what occurs from time to time here—

[Pages missing]

At present I believe we are safe. But truly do not know for how much longer.

Are you following this, I wonder? Or will you be lamenting the words of an ill mind, an old man driven insane at the end of his life. It is not so. I cannot tell what they will say of me. There are futures that I cannot see. Perhaps the best thing now is to tell you of my past. This may at last convince you.

Born to Mr and Mrs Nicholas Cecil Robinson-Deveraux, I was brought up in Marsh House for the first eleven years of my life. My mother, Felicia Durrant, came from a family whose roots stretched deep into the soil of Iders End and Essex. It was said that there had been Durrants in this part of the country since the Magna Carta or beyond. My maternal family were very proud of that.

In her youth, Felicia was comely but headstrong and outspoken, admiring of suffrage in an age when these qualities did not enhance the marital prospects of a young woman of means. Often on outings to Southend and Rochford she would make clear her views, offending any who were in the vicinity who raised objection to her modern take on politics, and once was known to chain herself to the Rochford Town Hall porch (there was a lack of railings to be found in the provincial market town). As a result, my grandfather, William Durrant, was, on several occasions, required to send his eldest daughter away for prolonged visits to his cousin, Hortence, in Belgravia, in the hope that time and absence might restore harmony to the regional status quo. During these 'holidays' my mother was introduced to the prominent esoteric philosophies of the age by her second cousin, Theodore, several years her senior. Whether it was true or merely posturing, Theodore professed to be part of several secret hermetic sects, including that known as the Golden Dawn.

It seemed Felicia was much taken by him. Not only was he endowed with handsome features, he was immensely charismatic and enhanced his air of mystery with a flamboyant cloak. Whether or not the feeling was mutual we shall never know. When Felicia returned from her trips, she seemed, as my grandfather once told me 'hectic' and unable to settle. She would go missing from the house for long hours and be found unconscious in various places around the island. Quite often in the grounds of the church. I have heard from others that my mother spent a great deal of time down in the village collecting folk tales, sketching the buildings and church.

She also took trips to book shops in Southend where she bought publications of rather a peculiar nature, encouraged no doubt by her Theodore.

One summer her cousin was invited to Marsh House to amuse Felicia and keep her mind occupied. Far from discouraging his daughter's interest in the arcane, my grandfather believed her new fixation to be a harmless distraction that might divert his daughter's gaze from the greater evil he perceived to be universal suffrage.

When Theodore requested the attendance of some of his old college friends, William Durrant agreed. They were to come for one night and be gone the next morning.

It was, apparently, my mother's and Theodore's intention to perform a great rite at midnight on the stage of the Our Lady's chapel. The inhabitants of Marsh House understood this to be some sort of play-acting and indulged the youths in their excitement, expressing their not entirely sincere wishes to see the 'show'. However, the Durrant household was promptly informed that the ritual to be undertaken required privacy and that they should continue their daily routine. A great relief to many of the servants.

Nobody knows exactly what happened down there that night. I have tried to talk to surviving villagers but there are not many who remember the event and some of what they recall is unclear.

The facts I have ascertained are these: at some point during the night a great fireball swept through the church, taking its roof off and destroying much of the interior, including the sacred window. A few of the young men and women from the village were involved and it was thought one of them, a boy of twenty, perished in the fire, though no remains were ever found.

Of course, my grandfather was enraged. The village too was distraught. Not only because of the boy, but also because of the partial destruction of their sacred church.

Theodore and his college friends fled back to London. Felicia was despatched abroad to finishing school.

My grandfather and his cousin, Hortence, were able to steer off further investigation, with a wedge of money given to the poor lad's family to compensate for the loss of their son. This may seem arbitrary but what good would have come of sending any of the young people to prison? The lad had gone to the church willingly and in any case there was no body to prove he was indeed deceased.

With some muttering this was accepted and the wider Durrant family embarked on a refurbishment of the church to further appease the people of Iders End. Although this was never completed in full.

After an event such as this it is difficult to silence tongues.

My grandfather despaired of my mother's prospects. Not only that, she was in danger of tarnishing the whole family. It was through a London friend that William Durrant was introduced to the man who would become my father. He was by then both an orphan and a widower and hardened to life. His comfort was found in the Presbyterian religion, which he embraced with much zeal and discipline. My grandfather believed him to be the right man to iron out his daughter's wayward tendencies. Her reputation had travelled, and she had not endeared herself to many men of society. Hence her marriage to my father necessitated a dowry of some weight. It was these lands and a significant amount of gold that finally tempted Mr Robinson-Deveraux into matrimony. My grandfather vacated these premises and bought a small villa on the south coast, nearer to my grandmother's family, which had been their wish for many years.

I believe the union was at first happy. Felicia was by all accounts enamoured of my father. Contemporaries have recalled a striking figure who was of good height with an athletic but sturdy build. His eyes were a conspicuous blue in colour and remained so right up till his death. I would imagine as a couple they turned many heads.

My father spoke to me only once of their early life together. His voice was warm as he recalled the first glimpse of my mother. She was, he said, 'a beauty, and sparkled too, within. Though now I wonder if it was the madness that burnt so brightly.'

Inevitably, my father did not feel comfortable with the people of Iders End and their superstitious ways. Not only did he halt the restoration of St Mary's, he knocked down the remains of the porch, with its pagan Sheela na gig. This was seen as an act of vandalism which caused much consternation in the village. The celebration of Lady's Day, or Modranicht as they called it, repelled him thoroughly. Villagers dressed up as animals to celebrate fecundity and congregated around the chapel for a service. The children would never be allowed, it was true, but what the grown men and women of the parish did sickened him. The very essence of pagan idolatry. Yet Felicia, a true child of the village, pointed out it was part of the fabric of their life. They were a remote community and progress was slow to find its way out to the mist-drenched Essex marshes. It would come in its own time and not that of her husband's. Forbidding their traditional customs, she claimed, would cause resentment and strengthen the villagers' resolve to practise where he could not see. This my father agreed upon to a certain extent, having experienced a sudden drop in the local supply of fresh food and able-bodied men for the fields immediately after the demolition of the porch.

Instead of banning the celebration, he bore down on the chapel, restricting its use to Sundays only and often took to the pulpit to sermonise himself in an attempt to bring reason to the rural unwashed.

In addition to this philosophical conflict he was also appalled by the bleak isolation and lack of civilised society. It was therefore not at all unexpected that my father reacted in the way he did to the events that were to shape all of our lives.

Despite his often prolonged absence (undoubtedly a mixture of both business and pleasure), I experienced a happy childhood with my older sister, Phoebe. And, although we were required to observe the occasional intervention of our well-meaning governess, Jane, much of our infancy was spent roaming the island with the children of the neighbouring farms. In many respects it was an idyllic start to our lives.

When my younger brother, Thomas, was born, Phoebe was packed off to a venerable boarding school. She was eleven and allegedly starting to display maternal characteristics: what my father referred to as 'a propensity towards the garrulous and an overburdening of confidence'.

Without my dear playmate I found myself alone. Mother was engaged with little Thomas so I was given much liberty to rove the islands.

Farmyards, fields, ditches, the seawalls, saltings and beaches became my vast playground and were the source of many adventures. In the winter the ponds would freeze and offer up the possibilities of skating or breaking ice – each as fun a pastime as the other. In spring, when the natural world began to stir, I would watch the bird life, which seemed to represent the whole of Britain, and the animals and search amongst the marine life and flotsam. Boxes and cargo that washed up in the creeks were endlessly fascinating and fired the imagination to consider the possibilities of foreign shores. I wonder if that may have inspired my eagerness in later life to travel. At harvest I would sneak out to find the other youngsters of the island, who congregated in the field behind the cars during mustard threshing, earning a few crafty coins from the farmers as we helped to glean the leftovers. At Easter I would help to de-mice the haystacks. This, I remember, involved hitting the stacks with a stick and then trapping the streaming mice as they scurried away. We would store their bodies till the end of the day when old Farmer Mathews would pay us a penny per score. And so too, do I have a memory of donning a mask and touring the farms and cottages of the villages, knocking on doors begging pennies or treats to celebrate the coming of Modranicht, of playing my part in the *stoning of the wren, which to my infant sensibility seemed little more than an overlong football match. It was natural for us to do these things.*

By and by the years passed and little Thomas grew from baby to child. He was a sweet boy and had a generous nature. Physically he resembled most my mother, with his curly locks the colour of wet wheat and the bluest of eyes. This resulted in his becoming favourite to my mother, a cause for much jealousy, though it was hardly Thomas's fault.

At the end of the holidays, when my preferred playmate, Phoebe, had been swept back to school, I would allow my little brother to accompany me on rambles. I believe there is not a tree left in Iders End that we did not climb. Often, we would set traps for water rats or explore the old blacksmith's forge, which had been abandoned at the end of the century, and provided a backdrop for many long games of pirates. At other times we would search the shore for unusual shells washed up from the deep sea or dredged by trawlers. While Thomas enjoyed these pursuits, perhaps driven by an unknown prescience, I often found he had gravitated back to the church at the bottom of the garden or to the creek beyond. Although adventurous in spirit, he seemed to prefer the solidity of the buildings and find solace in the shadows of the chapel.

Being so accustomed to the ways of the island, its ditches and tides (every child was well schooled in its patterns) I was fearless and, like most youngsters, impervious to the dangers of the wild. Though I started our travels with a keen eye on Thomas, as he gained in confidence, I relaxed my vigilance. To me with my ten years of experience he seemed perfectly able to take care of himself. Though he was but five, he was a serious little man and seemed so much older than his years. Certainly he displayed a more thoughtful demeanour than either myself or Phoebe. I have a vivid memory of him, hands on his knees, little face pinched into solemn concentration, by the creek gazing into a rock pool, stick in hand. I had a great fondness for him, but as I said, in the later months of that final year I failed to honour my duties as his protector. Something I intend to correct.

It was in December, of course, on one of our short days a-roaming that the vanishing occurred.

We had been exploring the creeks to the north of the house, attracted by the cries of the wintering birds: avocets, ringed plover, a variety of terns. I was absorbed in the observation of a nest when I first heard our governess call us to come inside. It was almost twilight by three o'clock then. But there was something so very exciting for a child to play in the darkness. And I was not ill-equipped. Jane, the governess, refused to let us outside at all unless we were fastened in to huge coats, balaclavas and gloves so thick you could barely move your fingers. Although play after sundown was strictly forbidden, I had managed to evade punishment on two occasions by exclaiming that I could not see where I was going and was promptly rewarded with my very own torch.

As I was absorbed by the fowl, I did what I had often done, and ignored Jane's call. My next interruption however was the bell for tea. I continued to pretend I had not heard it. But when the third bell rang it had an irritated edge to the peal so I responded relatively speedily.

I might add that, at this point, Thomas, though timid, was a ravenous child and I assumed that he had heeded the first call from Jane and had scrambled home ahead of me. This, I was to learn, was an incorrect assumption, for when I returned, I was interrogated as to Thomas's whereabouts. I told my mother truthfully that I had last seen my brother by the creek, whereupon I was scolded, and a servant, Mallory – my father's groom – was at once despatched to retrieve him.

Mallory, however, did not return promptly. Two hours later when I next saw him it was clear that fear was bright in his eyes. Though he had searched extensively by the creek, there was no trace of Thomas to be found. Very quickly the household and surrounding tenants burst into activity.

It was approaching midnight, as I understand it, that someone made the discovery of blood by the church. Not a great deal, and not, as was commonplace, on the altar. No, this was a fresh stain on the ruins of the anchoress's cell. My mother was thrown into a state of hysteria and was sedated. My father was sent a telegram.

I cannot remember much of the following few days, and it is really not of great significance. Father returned from London and despatched yet more searches, but to no avail. Phoebe's journey home was intercepted and she was sent instead to stay with our grandparents in the South. My mother's mental state grew weaker by the day until she gave up even venturing from her bedroom.

I spent my time unnoticed in the nursery, comforted by Jane, but almost rendered mute by guilt.

Christmas passed on to New Year. With no news of my little brother and the growing incapacitation of my mother, it was decided that I should go to boarding school. My father insisted I was approaching the right age for it and so by the end of January I found myself in Oxfordshire.

I did not return to Iders End until the summer, when I found the house much changed. My father was perpetually absent. Phoebe had joined our cousins on a tour of Europe so I was left alone with my mother, Felicia. The difference in her appearance was striking. Her eyes were sharp and quick but her face pallid and aged. Her hair had turned entirely grey. She spent much of her day in the village talking in murmurs with some of the old ones there, though she would lie to me and say she had been running errands or helping the wives.

Left to my own devices and supervised only by the kitchen staff, I went back to my lone roaming. A few times I spied her there, by the church, with the others. But I was too young to understand what it was all about.

In the evenings she would sit by the windows in the day room. A high round table was always positioned beside her. On top of it a lamp. Whatever the time of night, whatever the weather, she would keep the curtains open and, while she busied her fingers embroidering a sampler, she would sing out the window as if she was guiding someone back into the light.

It was an unusual and morbid atmosphere and in truth it was with some relief, when September came round again, that I packed my trunk for school. I did in fact enjoy school as much as I was able. I found comfort in the routine, and, having spent years building up stamina on my island treks, I became rather good at sports, which at last secured me some decent friends of my own. The atmosphere of order and brisk efficiency was a welcome relief to the strangeness of my home. So I was reluctant to return to Iders End for the next Christmas holiday.

It was now almost a year since Thomas had disappeared without trace and I knew I would be consumed with guilt and dread. However, when I did arrive back at Marsh House, I was greeted by Phoebe whom I had not seen in years. Only four years older than me, she seemed to have made the leap from tomboy into young woman. However, she had retained her vibrancy and was still full of life. I was exceptionally pleased to see her.

Mother too was transformed. She had tidied her hair up and although there was a forced gaiety in everything she seemed to do, I found a solid optimism within. Phoebe confided that mother was looking forward to a gift she was to receive. Apparently we would all delight in it. 'Wheels had been set in motion,' she had told Phoebe. And the gift was 'already coming back'.

My first night home, we put up decorations and were even allowed to erect a pine tree. My father did not approve of what he saw as a pagan practice. But as he was not due back until the 23rd, my mother insisted we observe the tradition.

Phoebe and I busied ourselves buying presents and made several trips into Southend to get ingredients for our Christmas Feast. Mother was insistent that everything should be perfect this year. It was perhaps an unusual stance for a grieving parent but Phoebe and I were both grateful for it. We journeyed around the county visiting relatives and friends and received our southern cousins. Of the days leading up to Christmas Eve and Lady's Day I can recall flurries of activity, company and a large measure of fun.

However, when father came home this was all to change. The night he returned I was asleep in the nursery but roused by raised voices. Upon hearing a crash I started and went out into the hallway where I found Phoebe padding up the stairs. Shushing me, she put her finger to her lips and showed me back to bed.

The next day we saw the Christmas tree had been removed. Though my father seemed more distant than usual he made a fuss of my sister and me and took us shooting that day down by the creek.

After dinner Phoebe and I retired to our bedrooms, inevitably excited by the promise of Christmas Eve. I know I had found it difficult to sleep but had eventually dropped off, only to be woken at midnight by the front doorbell.

Hearing shouts and a commotion, I once again went out onto the hallway and saw Phoebe at the foot of the stairs. Descending to meet her a most unusual sight came into view. My father and Mallory were in the act of restraining a young man with a mop of the lightest blond hair and glittering graphite eyes. As I came to the foot of the stairs, the lad, who must only have been Phoebe's age, stopped short, blinking furiously at me. His face broke out into a beatific smile that seemed at once to convey both fear and relief. Mallory used his momentary stillness to pull his arms tighter behind him. The boy yelped then cried out, 'Edward, thank you. It is I, Thomas. See your brother. I am saved.'

Dumbstruck I stood rooted to the spot. The young fellow was much older than me. Thomas had celebrated his fifth birthday but six months before he vanished. This boy was at least ten years older. I looked deeper into his face. His eyes were of a similar shape to my younger brother's, but grey where Thomas's had been blue, his hair silvery blond, when Thomas's was honeyed. At that point my mother came screaming from the upper floor. When she reached the foot of the stairs, she stopped, surveyed the lad and then did something none of us could have imagined. She ordered my father and his groom to release the boy. Then she embraced him and led him away into the house.

My recollections of what happened thereafter have not remained intact. I know there were terrible arguments between my parents that seemed to go on for days. For the first time in many years the Lady's Day procession was not allowed to go ahead. This caused further consternation in the village.

Eventually my father stormed from Marsh House.

The new boy was then taken into the household and given a room adjoining my mother's. On New Year's Day Phoebe and I were returned to our separate schools. I would not return to Iders End for fifty-two years.

Although they did not divorce, my father took up a house in London and thereafter it was to this address that Phoebe and I returned in school holidays.

I never saw my mother again.

My father would not speak of her nor answer our questions. Phoebe and I were able only to surmise the following from the scraps we were able to garner from friends and servants. The young boy I had seen in the hallway attested to be our lost brother. As ludicrous as that may have been, my mother believed him so.

It was my father's conviction that the boy had insinuated himself into the favours of my mother with the help of one of the household servants. For Felicia insisted that he knew things about her that no one else could, that he shared Thomas's birthmark and that she had worked hard to bring him back.

What the third of her remarks meant, nobody knew.

Eventually, in some despair, my father attempted to have her committed to an asylum. It was only the intervention of his father-in-law that prevented this tragic outcome. Whilst my father may have been coaxed into enduring an insane spouse, he could not tolerate the presence of what he called the 'changeling' child. At one point the lad was taken into custody in Shoebury police station but once again my grandfather stepped in to negotiate a settlement. Seeing that Felicia was determined not to give up her folly, my father abandoned her to Marsh House, signing the estate over and, thereafter, permanently removed to London with his two remaining children.

Consequently, Phoebe and I went from confusion to a gradual acceptance of our situation and thought less and less of our time in the country. Whilst not a doting parent, my father made sure we were well fed, well educated and checked every year by a range of doctors for any signs of hereditary insanity. As the years progressed, we became accustomed to our lifestyle in London and as we reached adulthood appreciated the social aspect of town living from which we would have been excluded if we were back in Essex.

When I was sixteen war broke out on the continent. 1939. Like most of my peers I was prevented from enlisting at first. Many thought it would be done in a year. But once that landmark had passed we became aware of the struggle and I persuaded my father to allow me to sign up.

Before I went away to war Phoebe was wed. A nice young fellow, name of William Isaacs. Their marriage took place one week before he was called up and two months before he was killed. If I had known that Phoebe was pregnant I would not have left her behind. But at the time I did not and retrospect is no aid to solace so I will write of it no more. The war was a sordid and unspeakable affair. My recollections are too vast and appalling to go into here and besides it is not my purpose to describe them. Others have done more justice. Suffice it to say at the conclusion of the war I returned to find our London house bombed. My father and Mallory had refused to 'cower in the shelters' and had been taken too. Phoebe and her son, Howard, were in Surrey at the time with my father's parents and chose to remain there for the duration of the war and thereafter.

I was to some extent traumatised by what I had seen and felt little connection to London or indeed England. When I was offered a position in Morocco with the consulate, I jumped at the chance to experience another kind of life. Rabat was indeed a salve without associations and with a temperate climate, and so I spent many years there. It was the first of many such positions. I was willing to move frequently so was promoted through the hierarchy. A memorable life, but not one in which I laid down many roots.

I returned home from time to time. That is, I returned to wherever Phoebe resided with my nephew. Little Howard Isaacs was a lovely child with a sunny outlook, as cheery as his mother had once been.

In 1950, however, Phoebe married again. Her second husband, Donald Rabeson, made her happy but did not entirely endear himself to me. I found him a weasly type of chap, with pink eyes and a thin moustache. Shortly after their wedding they moved further to the west where Donald was developing a business near the Cotswolds. I visited her, the last time, in 1958, when Howard was turning into a strapping young man. She seemed very happy. I can still recall how we sat in her garden and sipped white wine finding some time to ourselves. Phoebe asked me if I had heard from our mother. I was dumbstruck. We had not spoken of her since the year we had left Iders End when, after expecting communication from her and finding none, we resolved not to speak of her again. I shook my head and asked her why she had asked. Phoebe told me she had received a letter of apology from Felicia, expressing her regret. Our father had, according to the writer, banned her from making contact with us, threatening her with internment should she breach the agreement.

I asked my sister what she was going to do. She replied slowly that she didn't yet know and then said, 'She says she has already spoken with you.'

Protesting that this was not the case, I declared I had had no communication with our mother since the day we left the village. Phoebe accepted my answer, but I saw for the first time suspicion in her eyes. It was a shame that the spectre of doubt had cast its shadow over that weekend, for only nine months later my poor dear sister was dead to cancer.

It was a terrible blow.

I attempted to stay in touch with Donald, but neither of us had much inclination to see each other regularly and by the mid-sixties we had drifted out of touch.

I endeavoured to keep up with Howard, however. For I was his only living relative.

I went to Howard's wedding to the lovely Pamela of whom I approved thoroughly. I also attended the christenings of his two children, Joshua and Luke, and sporadic family gatherings, though my work abroad did not allow for regular visits.

I was informed, in 1987, that I had come into possession of Marsh House. My mother had died some years earlier and there had been problems tracking me down. The changeling, as my father once called him, had expired a year prior to my mother.

I knew not what to expect and so it was curiosity more than anything that led me back to my childhood home.

In contrast to London, Iders End seemed to have withstood any change whatsoever. The farms and ditches and creeks and inn and cottages and fields, were all there, almost exactly as they had been the day I had said goodbye to them, New Year's Day in 1935.

The house was in good working order and seemed to me to present a sanctuary from the modern life in London, which now seemed so strange. I promptly moved into it, acquired a housekeeper and the rest is history.

Or will be.

As I moved around and reintegrated with the village, many of my childhood memories returned. And, perhaps for the first time in decades, I started to contemplate in more detail the story of Thomas.

I must tell you now that the more I learned of this exceptional piece of land, its mysteries and unique qualities, the more I began to wonder if my mother had been right to do the things she did, to take the lad into the house. My intuitions began to take hold more strongly when I observed something uncanny down by the anchoress's cell as we approached Lady's Day.

I had decided to take up watercolours and thought I might preserve some of the history of the place in a visual medium.

Having sketched the old boathouse and the church from a distance, I gave in to an impulse to commit the cell to canvas, it being of some historical significance here.

I remember that day in detail – setting up my canvas, mixing my colours carefully and beginning with the sky. It was always so easy here. Vast swathes of marble strewn with streams of angry blue-grey glowered heavily at the trees beneath. The outposts of the orchard stood protectively about the chapel walls, taking the brunt of the south-westerly wind.

Emerging from the side of the chapel, like a hasty extension that had been thought better of, was the anchoress's cell. I recall considering the rocks and stones that dotted the main rectangle of the cell: ancient, eroded by age and mould. My gaze flitted from canvas to cell then back again, attempting to replicate the shades and form of the chapel, the broken wall, halting at the top. Here the air seemed to have thickened. When my eyes returned to the cell, I sighted a small furry ball, two feet or so to the right of the cell, that had not been there a moment before. After a few minutes it began to uncurl and I recognised the spiky quills of a rather oddly coloured hedgehog: a pale snowy face peeked out from leached amber quills. Unstretching on all fours, it sniffed the ground and orientated itself northeast, in the direction of the tightly interwoven hedge of blackthorn and hazel that bordered the churchyard. I remember thinking the little fellow would have to get over to it soon and go back to his hibernating sleep. It was mid-winter. I watched it crawl unevenly across the graveyard, then returned my eyes to the cell. Now, it looked to me like the air there was warping, as if willing itself to form a smog. It was too difficult to capture in paint – I was a beginner after all – so instead I turned to the grass. Damp green patches gave way to hard mud where many feet had worn a path across to the cell. A fluttering sound pulled my eyes from it, and I saw that a sparrow had perched in the hawthorn hedge. I remember wondering if I might use the image of the bird to animate the painting and enhance the composition and accidentally dropped my palette. The sparrow caught fright and took off from the branch, heading away towards the cell. I watched it fly in a *quick straight line over the boulders then abruptly the sparrow disappeared in mid-air.*

I could not believe it, so got up and made an inspection of the cell to see if it was somewhere within. But it was not. Of course I thought it a discrepancy in my own brain. And later that week I made an appointment with Doctor Good.

We had been friends as children and both remembered our times in the fields with warmth. After a brief conversation about our circumstances he insisted I should come over to dinner at his house in Wakering. Of course I accepted and we got on to the business of my concern. I recounted my experience.

Doctor Good listened carefully and then did two things. First he wrote a letter to Southend Hospital commending me to a neurological specialist 'to put your mind at ease, for I am sure that there is nothing amiss'. The second thing was most surprising: he told me I should speak with Abel Gardner, the landlord at the Half Moon, though he would not speak of it further. He said he would elaborate when I dined with him.

Of course, I was most intrigued by this, and that night I made my way down to the inn. Abel was busy and it was not till we approached the end of the evening that I was able to

[Page missing]

'The same as your brother, Thomas,' he said. 'Well, he come out didn' he?'

My mind was still reeling from what he had inferred so I merely nodded.

'Age he was, your mother reckoned it had been ten years before. Think it took him sometime to work out what was going on. But there was someone there, waiting for him. Who helped.' He narrowed his eyes and glared at me, speaking with purpose. 'An older man.'

I tried to gauge his meaning but could not.

'Well, it's that place, innit,' he said with a glint. 'The cell. Sometimes you go in and you don't come back out again. Not in the same "now".'

Part of me wanted to believe that the man had lost his mind. Though the connections were being made internally.

'Time – it's a special thing,' Abel murmured. 'The sacrifice keeps the soil fertile. You know what we're like with our ways down here. We like time, all right. Have lots of fun with it. Just don't like it moving on, changing things.'

He could see that I wasn't convinced so he wrote down an address and told me to visit it. That if I did, all would become clear.

I left that night with grave misgivings, but the

following day I resolved to put an end to my confusion, to clear things up once and for all.

I went to the address.

[pages missing]

The inordinate experience of that meeting, I cannot commit to words.

Suffice it to say the shock of revelation, once it had subsided, transformed into an uneasy understanding of the nature of the phenomenon.

Why it happens here – I do not know … not for one minute do I believe my mother or Theodore caused it to occur for the first time. I do however believe they reawakened something that had perhaps lain dormant till then.

There is no need to rationalise this.

It will not work.

Just keep an open mind: some things can't be explained.

*Or perhaps, that is, they can't be explained **yet**.*

I am pleased mother and Thomas were happy. In many ways I look forward to seeing them again.

I should say no more now, other than to advise you – soon you will take your own leap of faith. You will know when it presents itself to you. You must take it. So much rests on it. Don't be afraid.

So, my friend, we are come to Lady's Day, or as is its

ancient name, Modranicht. I can hear them assembling at the church. It has already begun. I should ready myself for my own leap: I must take care of Thomas when he emerges, confused and alone. I should repay my debt: this time, I will not shirk my duties.

If I am right, my body will not be found. This may make it difficult for Howard's son. But what will be, I know now, will be. I suppose, should I be wrong about any of this, should it not work out as I imagine, then I would like to be buried under the hawthorn tree overlooking the creek, where I can continue my observations of the universe.

Be strong, my dear.

Fortune favours the brave.

Good luck,

Cecil Robinson-Devereaux

III

~~THIRD MAGUS~~

FIRST MAGGIE: THE ANCHORESS

At first there was only blackness. Then I became aware that within it, bright sparks were flitting about like a blizzard, curling into a spiral around me.

I had the impression of movement though couldn't tell which way was which.

And my body was restricted.

There was no space.

At one point it was as if I had turned into something of an updraft and saw a patch of black a distance away, the luminous bulb of the moon crossing the darkness like a comet. It disappeared out of sight and murkiness crowded round, lightening, becoming grey. Bubbling clouds boiled and pitched in the gap, receded and moved away, becoming smaller, merging into the light. Then darkness again

– the moon darting west to east, light, sun, clouds, black, light.

Light inside and out.

Freefalling into endless white light.

Then, a thud, and I was here.

I was in my new 'now'.

The Middle Age isn't all it's cracked up to be, let me tell you. Although, at the same time, there is a strong possibility that I might have simply gone mad. Or perhaps still be dreaming. In the void.

In fact, when I first came round that was exactly what I was thinking – man, one hell of a dream!

But it went on for ages.

And I do mean that.

Dark ages.

I kind of *knew* I was in the cell, I just couldn't work out how it had been rebuilt so quickly.

It wasn't as bare as when I'd seen it. Quite cosy for the time, I suppose, with sheep furs on the walls, straw on the ground, some sort of sacking that was full of wool for a bed, woven rugs, and a fire going in the corner. The toilet was like something you'd find in the Glastonbury Green Field, but it was better than nothing.

Took some getting used to though. As did the festivals. Oh my god. They have so many – Ash Wednesday, Lent, Palm Sunday, Easter, Ascension, All Saints Day (they haven't really got to grips with Halloween yet), Christmas, Rogationtide. It goes on. And on.

Still does.

The food's not great. Thank god, they've discovered salt, otherwise I'd not be able to keep it down at all. I do my best though – and I've suggested some recipes, and tried to impose more order and experimentation with the herb garden. I'm proud to have talked them through a poultice of mint leaves and water and to have introduced the concept of cleaning your teeth. They weren't sure about this in the beginning, but they appreciate the fresher breath, I'm sure. Now we're working on an early prototype toothbrush from twigs and boiled sheep's wool.

Communication isn't great – Early English is like another language, but there are hints of French. I got my GCSE and now I've been here a while, I can just about get on.

They're attentive though, eager to please, and they treat me like a goddess.

Which, to all intents and purposes, I am.

Bestowed with a knowledge that seems to the populace nothing short of miraculous, my reputation as a wise woman has traversed the realm. I have many visitors seeking answers. Quite often I can help out in that regard. My years spent in the offices of a medical publisher have paid off. It's amazing what you can pick up subconsciously. In fact, I sometimes wonder if that's why I was chosen? Why Pete took my hand and led me over to the altar that Modranicht. Or maybe it's something else that Hattie and Luke told him. I wouldn't know. So there's no point trying.

What I do know is how to diagnose some of the ailments the villagers present to me – colds, flu, viruses, chicken pox, broken limbs, concussion, sprains and so on. I advise upon treatments as best as I can: quarantine is 'solitary prayers', bandages and splints are 'bindings to God'. I ad lib. You've got to work with the lingo. Of course there's a lot of ailments that I'm clueless about. Which is probably good, or else there's always the possibility that I could be accused of witchcraft and strung up before the year's out. And that would not be a good outcome at all.

I've asked for books to read to pass the time, though Gutenberg is not yet a twinkle in his great, great, great, great, great-grandma's eye. They've got hold of some manuscripts and so I'm going through them. In fact, me and Ivo, the cleric, are spending evenings reading them aloud.

And yes, Ivo is quite fit in a kind of regressive Dark Ages kind of way. Raven hair, sultry eyes and as tall as these men get, which is about one inch taller than my own good self. I'm going to have to do something about those lice at some point, but right now, the chap is providing more than adequate solace. Medieval boys aren't slow on the uptake.

He's coming over tonight for a bit of a 'read', and I'm moving the relationship on so that at some point he'll help get me out.

See, I remember what Hattie said: we, myself and Ivo, will run away this year. At some point we will return. Then we'll leave again. And I guess that's where this cell comes in. Who knows where it will vomit us out?

I don't mind.

It's definitely time to move on.

Time for a change.

Time and tides wait for no one.

Time. It sure is a funny thing.

TWO MINDS

It was the way he looked at the table, when they walked into the murder house, that gave Inspector Drew Oates the first indication that something was not quite right. And murder house wasn't quite right either. It was, if one was going to be particular, a murder flat. Apartment really. Stylish and swish, though small.

If you could afford to live in this part of town you would only ever end up with 'petite and bijou'. But if she was going to be a pedant about this, and it was an accusation that stung her from time to time, it was when they walked into the murder *room*.

The timing, Inspector Oates had noticed, was quite a coincidence. She'd said as much to her sergeant when the call came in to attend a burglary on Wimslow Street, less than one day after the heist in Diamond Street, a mere four blocks away. It hadn't been a murder house at that point, just a burglar's paradise.

Diamond Street wasn't the actual address of the road, more of a nickname used by those in the know to insinuate the hierarchy of jewellers it was synonymous with. Gowton Gardens, as it was formally identified, was the epicentre of the district, the home of prestige jewellers, one-stop-shops for rock stars' multiple engagement rings, safety deposit boxes for the comfortably paranoid and secure vaults for the excessively wealthy. Lower-ranking lapidaries and start-ups were located on its fringes in the shadows of the street's glittering edifices. Of course, these premises came with highly evolved, state-of-the-art security technologies. And more than a sprinkling of low-fi, fleshy guardians clad in distinguished uniforms with tassels and braiding, who contributed much to the manufactured glamour of the place. So the discovery yesterday of the theft of several million pounds' worth of finely crafted pieces from one of the most respected emporiums was not just a blow to the heart of *Lawrence the Jewellers* but sent shockwaves through the entire city. One troubling aspect, as yet to be revealed to the press, was that the alarm to the local station had been fused, potentially disabled with intent. The back-up security firm entrusted with responding had also assumed a malfunction. For, being a bank holiday and an unusually pleasant one at that, the zero-hours watchman and his zero-hours skeleton crew had merely added the job to the list of calls to be logged and keys to be turned on their next security lap.

This litany of bad judgements and its resulting disaster called into question the hitherto lauded and impregnable fortitude of the multi-billion-pound institution of Diamond Street.

It was inevitable that the rumour mill would spring to attention and set off at some speed. Already a few of its peddlers were suggesting an inside job. And that was a real concern. One that Inspector Oates was made aware of via text messages from the commissioner herself, as well as various traders, a Chinese ambassador, two MPs, one minor royal and the prime minister, whose mistress had a penchant for sapphires. A swift conclusion was essential, preferable and might well make Oates promotable.

Not that the lure of promotion swayed her especially. Inspector Oates prided herself on a good clean-up rate despite the fact that she had been consistently overlooked since her last promotion twelve years since. Her career, she had resigned herself, like the heavy mortgage on her flat, would be nothing but a steady uphill slog. The force's selection board evidently favoured applicants who were younger, brighter, networked more efficiently, who were media-trained, photogenic and sometimes flexible. Like her sergeant, Daryl MacFall, who was all these things, and yet still a dunderhead. Though mostly he covered his failings well, equipped as he was with a ferret-like instinct that guided him, like a meteor, towards those he should court, those with whom he might play golf and win against and those to whom he should lose. And unlike the old adage, Oates observed, flattery seemed to get MacFall almost everywhere.

It semi-surprised her, therefore, that the young officer was so eager to accompany her today – she, Inspector Oates, a well-known 'plodder'.

She'd said, 'Stay here and continue with statements.'

But he shook his head and fetched his coat. 'Two minds are so much better than one,' he called over his shoulder.

Inspector Oates supposed he was right. Perhaps this was, she ruminated in the car, an attempt on MacFall's part to reinsert himself into her good books. Of which he had fallen out several times over the past few months on account of too frequently going AWOL. Radio silence from inferiors was something Inspector Oates could not abide. Second only to the use of the insulting nickname given to her good self, which she had banned from her squad. It compared her to an unflattering older fictional female detective, a doddery old codger from the imagination of Ms Christie, when in fact she reckoned herself more of a Jennifer Hart. Though peppered with grey now, Drew had once sported a flaming mane that was not entirely dissimilar to Stephanie Powers' in her youth. Oh, how she had loved *Hart to Hart*. In fact, it was this whodunnit series that had lit the tinder stick that consequently ignited her passion for doing what was right. And doing what was right for a living seemed the best way to live one's life. Or so she had once thought.

Her career had turned out to be not as simple as that. Like the state of her hair, more shades of grey had found their way in. Reporting MacFall for his tardiness being one of them. So she had sent a trusted colleague into the canteen to make some gentle enquiries. A new love interest was the consensus.

Inspector Oates thought long and hard and decided that, rather than inform HR he was distracted and not pulling his weight, she would talk to the sergeant instead. It was unacceptable, she had discovered, to grass on colleagues in this particular constabulary, even if they revealed themselves to be thoroughly bad apples. She'd watched enough *Line of Duty* to know this never ended well, and had learned the hard way, in her last interview for promotion, that nobody loves a snitch or a goody-two-shoes.

For, when asked to describe the top quality required to become a Chief Inspector, she voiced in earnest the word that had popped into her mind: 'Integrity.'

It clearly wasn't at the forefront of her superintendent's. 'Loyalty,' he snapped. 'Loyalty binds us. Far more effective even than a quick cuff round the ears.'

'In a cell?' she dared. 'When the prisoner is restrained?'

'Loyalty,' he repeated.

She didn't get that job. Nor the next.

Or the one after that.

Which is why a stern reprimand in The Grapes, the week prior to the heist, had been delivered to MacFall over a pint. And, fair play, ever since he *had* upped his game, returning to his former 'eager beaver' persona, even polishing himself off a bit and buying a new suit. Inspector Oates had to give him credit for that. And just as well really, as over the past few days the local felons seemed intent on making their hometown a contender for crime capital of the world.

The inspector glanced at her sergeant now as he scanned the scene before them. MacFall's face was quizzical, his ears keened like a bat navigating at night.

Reluctant to enter though, she noticed. This was no time for dilly-dallying. 'Come on then,' she urged, and he scampered to attention.

The sergeant sniffed the empty hall. Inside, the air felt tense, as if it was waiting for something to happen or sensed a predator nearby. Oates's senses heightened too. She said rather unoriginally, 'Careful now,' and together they padded down the corridor.

When they turned into the living room MacFall gasped. Loudly.

'Bloody hell,' he said.

And he was quite right. For there was much of the stuff puddling on the carpet, staining the coffee table and saturating the couch.

The victim appeared not to have struggled despite the handle of a knife protruding from her chest. The front of her shirt was soaked a deep aubergine and her chalky face, which had lolled back onto the sofa as her life had leaked away, wore an expression that Oates thought looked like astonishment. Her eyes were glassy and wide, brows arched, mouth wide open. Why astonishment? She thought. Why not horror? Fear? Panic?

'Put your gloves on,' ordered the inspector firmly as MacFall reached towards a glass on the coffee table. Tsk, tsk, she thought. If he wasn't careful he'd leave fingerprints all over the show.

Warned, he shrank back. 'Sorry. I wasn't thinking. Looks like she had company. See.'

An empty bottle of champagne stood between two flutes.

She watched him withdraw a pair of latex gloves from a pocket.

'Did you touch it?' the inspector growled. 'The bottle?'

'I don't know. Maybe brushed past. I was going to point out *that*.' He took a pen from his pocket and lifted a discarded lanyard by its thin, ribbon-like strap. 'Staff ID, *Lawrence the Jewellers*.'

Inspector Oates nodded. 'She was an employee then. Did you interview her about the robbery?'

'Phoned in sick,' said MacFall, his eyes fixed on the corpse. 'Better call it in.' And his hand zipped straight to his pocket and began to fish around.

'I'll do it.' The inspector stopped him with a gesture and removed her own mobile from her bag. 'You go and check there's no one else here.'

But MacFall didn't move. His colour had gone.

Inspector Oates followed his gaze and saw his focus had fallen on a phone. Blood had splashed and dried into a rusty colour on the screen, so it did look rather grisly.

Though they'd both seen much worse.

'Must be hers,' her sergeant said eventually, attempting a more casual tone than his body language suggested.

'No,' returned Oates. 'Left hand.' And she directed him to the poor corpse on the couch, stunned and surprised, still clutching her phone. 'She didn't have time to call for help.'

'Then whose mobile is this …?'

'Her guest's,' said the inspector. 'Must have been disturbed and not had time to clean up. I would hazard it's an accomplice who turned the tables on her. Sloppy though – leaving the phone like that.'

'I wonder why he'd do that?' said MacFall, nervily.

'He?' questioned Oates and eyed her colleague. 'People will do anything if the price is high enough. Nice little semi out of the smoke.' Pay off your mortgage. 'A couple of all-inclusives on the Costa

Brava.' Goodbye working bank holidays. 'Early retirement.' No more struggling for promotion. 'New suit.'

His miniature eyes snapped to hers.

'There's a lot you can do with that amount of money,' she said and pulled out her mobile. 'I can't say I wouldn't be tempted.'

He held his breath for a moment then said, 'Would you?'

'A-ha,' she thought a moment later, but she had to be sure, and so she started dialling a number.

'Who are you calling?' MacFall took a step.

The inspector caught a sudden whiff of death, tinged with something rooty and feral. Her nostrils flared. 'Back up,' she said tartly.

They both jumped as the phone on the coffee table burst into life.

Beneath arterial spatter the illuminated screen was visible. 'Marple calling,' it read.

'Right, that does it,' Inspector Oates wearily sank a sigh three-quarters full of duty and a quarter of regret.

'You know,' she said to MacFall the dunderhead. 'For a second there, I was in two minds.'

CHRISTMAS DAY AT THE ESSEX WITCH MUSEUM

To be honest, I hadn't built my hopes up. Who had? The country was in the eye of an almighty storm. Luckily Sam and I had decided to tie ourselves to the mast of the Witch Museum and see out the pandemic together in Adder's Fork.

Bronson, ever practical, made the decision to cut his losses and move in with us at the Witch Museum, so he could continue to do his job (get paid) and have some company on Christmas Day. As he said, 'It won't be the greatest, but I've had worse. Like when our submarine sank to the bottom of the ocean. That was a Christmas I don't want to remember.'

I decided to take that as a compliment, times were hard – you had to grab them when you could. I borrowed a caravan off Bob Acton, and had it towed to the grounds of the museum so that Bronson could quarantine. Thing is, he enjoyed the 'self-sufficiency' so much that he announced he was going to stay there throughout the Yuletide season. It was no skin off my nose and meant that I could offer the spare bedroom to our museum 'bubble household'. This consisted of Auntie Babs and Uncle Del. True, you were meant to be in a single household with a child under the age of eighteen, but Babs had registered Del as 'learning impaired' so while the authorities were working out that one, we were able to see each other, which was kind of nice.

Everything's relative, right?

And I mean that in many ways.

Anyway, they came over on Christmas Eve with a trailer full of their latest grocery delivery, which contained enough alcohol to restock the village shop ten times over. Praise the Lord. There had been a rush on the shops since all the lorry drivers got stuck outside Dover and I'd been worried that people were going to get on the same vibe as me and replace lettuce with wine. We were, however, good to go. Auntie Babs said that Christmas had no business with salads anyway. I tended to agree with that train of thought.

We'd dotted a few festive decorations around the Witch Museum, but, given the situation, it all had a bit of a hollow ring. In the end, we concentrated our efforts on a nice big pine in the dining room-cum-office and stowed all our gifts under it.

After they arrived, Babs put the turkey in to cook overnight, which was a relief as, although I am a goddess in many ways, I'm glad to report that I am thoroughly undomesticated. Well, perhaps not 'thoroughly' – I managed to prepare chipolatas and the stuffing. Bronson attended to the sprouts and whipped up a 'no-cook' Italian desert. Sam did the spuds with Del, then Babs chased everyone out of the kitchen and announced it was time to exchange one present each.

To be honest, I hadn't been feeling it. Probably I should have kept my thoughts to myself. But I've never been very good at that, so I went a bit teenage and pouty and said, 'Really? I can't be bothered. The fun's gone out of it. Doesn't feel like Christmas this year.'

Everyone sighed.

Babs said we should be counting our blessings.

Del said, 'Amen to that.'

Sam asked Alexa to play 'It's Beginning to Look a Lot Like Christmas'.

'Come on,' he said. 'Try and loosen up a bit.'

Which shows you how bad I'd gottten as a) my curator was not known for his laid-back attitude, and

b) normally I was the first person dancing on top of the pub table.

I sat down and swung my feet up and sighed. 'Sorry, you're right.'

Auntie Babs, who was wearing an apron printed with a semi-naked muscle-man, a sprig of mistletoe peeping from his thong, tutted and said, 'Show some decorum. Get those boots off the table, Mabel.'

I was wearing new, gold cowboys which had been a present to myself, and although I hadn't taken them outside yet, I supposed they might be a bit germy, so did as I was told and composed myself more neatly.

'Now,' said Babs. 'I suppose you're right – we haven't got into the true spirit of it yet. But we'll change right now. We all know Christmas is really about presents. The more the merrier!'

I noted the moral dichotomy in her statement but could not muster the energy to point it out.

'Think of the little Baby Jesus and the Three Kings of Orient Spa – the season is all about the gifts. Big ones, little ones, expensive ones…' Babs chimed softly and eyed the Christmas tree.

'And spending time with the ones you love,' said Uncle Del and sent his wife the sweetest smile.

'Presents,' said Auntie Babs firmly.

I wasn't going to be a pooper so I made some positive-sounding grunting noises, and within a few minutes the others came and gathered round the table. Auntie Babs popped a cork on some bubbly and then I took four presents from under the tree and gave Uncle Del one from me. Two pairs of socks and a bottle of whisky, which I hoped we would drink together.

'Oh thanks, Rosie dear,' he said and blew me a kiss. None of us were getting close to each other, bubble or not.

Del gave Sam a gift pack of Old Spice, which Sam received with a wince, although he camouflaged his expression quickly into a super-wide grin, and hurriedly passed Auntie Babs a heavy rectangular package.

We could all tell it was a book.

Luckily it was portraits of fifties pin-ups, which she appreciated. Thank God.

All eyes turned to me.

Babs handed over her present. It was floppy. I unwrapped it and took out a T-shirt that read 'We are the daughters of the women you couldn't burn.'

'It's surly, feminist and a bit witchy woo,' she said. 'Got you written all over it. Nice and tight across the chest too – a girl's got to show off her assets.'

Sam coughed, and coloured. I knew what was getting his goat – the old pedant was going to say something about the text and right on cue he trotted out. 'But they mostly hanged them here and in the US.'

'So maybe,' I said, 'it should read "We are the daughters of the women you couldn't hang".'

'Mmm,' said Auntie Babs. 'Do you know what I think is stronger? And maybe more truthy …'

We all replied we didn't. I glared at Sam to not correct her English.

'What about this?' she said. '"Actually, we *are* the daughters of the women that you hanged."'

'Oooh,' I said. 'That's good. A lot of them did have children. I mean it's not good that they had children and that they were then orphaned, but the idea of the children growing up and wreaking vengeance, I do like.'

'I'd omit the "actually",' Sam said.

'Oh my good lord,' said Uncle Del. 'I don't know where you get it from, Babs. I really don't. That's too scary by 'arf.'

'It is,' I said, nodding slowly at my aunt. 'Definitely more effective.' I caught Sam's eye. 'Let's do a T-shirt for the Witch Museum.'

He nodded silently – he liked it.

'You be sure to let everyone know it's my copyright,' said Auntie Babs. 'Now bugger off. Don't come back before 2.30. Then its dinner, the Queen's speech and tipsy parlour games, you know how I do like my games. Hop it.'

So we all duly wrapped up and waddled out of the museum into the lane.

We were halfway up the High Road, near the playing fields, when we caught sight of something on the main road.

I say we, but it was essentially Uncle Del who said, 'Stone the crows – what's that then? A bleedin' horse?'

I thought he was joking and laughed. But as we got closer we saw that it was, in fact, a donkey. It had two long, dark, grey ears and a brownish coat with a white belly. Under its feet was a motionless baby.

Well, not a real one – a crumpled plastic doll.

'Most perplexing,' said Sam when we got there, which pretty much summed it up for everyone.

Bronson caught hold of the donkey's lead rope and gave it a pat on the head. When it had moved a couple of steps towards him, out of kicking distance, Sam bent down to inspect the damaged toy.

While he was down there I took the opportunity to surreptitiously inspect the curator's rear. Yep – all looked trim and well formed. Say what you like about Sam and his bossy, irritating ways – the man was exceedingly fit and had a rather delightful derrière. I really couldn't help but linger.

Uncle Del coughed at me and tutted.

I took my eyes away from Sam's butt and pretended to be outraged.

That was good timing anyway, because Sam had picked up the doll and spun round to show me. It was a balding Tiny Tears that had wet its nappy several times, lost an arm and been chewed around the left leg. Barbaric, even for a doll.

'Oh look, it's three wise men, a donkey and a baby,' a hoarse voice erupted. 'But that ain't no Virgin Mary I'm seeing, for sure.'

'Thank you, Tone,' I said when I had located the source of the insult.

The youngest member of the Bridgewater clan was sitting in the bus shelter, heaving his shoulders up and down and coughing out a suspicious-smelling plume of smoke.

We went over to see him with the donkey in tow.

'Know anything about this then, young Tone?' asked Bronson and waggled the lead rope.

Tone sucked his lips. 'I been trying to work out if it's really there.' His eyes were very bloodshot.

'How long have you been sitting in the shelter?' asked Sam.

'I dunno,' Tone said. 'Come out to have a toke, free of Granddad. He's becoming quite a stoner.'

Del let out a little gasp, but Tone smiled, 'Helps with his arthritis, Granddad says.'

Bronson sighed. 'Well, that don't help us much with the donkey.'

'No,' said Tone philosophically. 'True.'

'Any ideas where it might have come from?' I asked.

'Not a scooby.'

'Mmm,' I said. 'Donkeys and babies. We should try the church.'

Everyone agreed, so we all turned our attentions towards St Michael's. Tone decided to come along for a ride and tried unsuccessfully to get on the donkey.

Del muttered something about not getting too close.

Tone coughed.

Del told him to do it into his elbow.

Tone said he hadn't got Covid.

Del said you couldn't be too careful, then went and walked over the other side of the road.

Tone yelled over that he *was* being careful because of his granddad.

Del told him not to shout as that could propel infected 'aerosol particles' for metres.

Tone muttered something unclear about Del being a total aerosol, and so to avoid any further escalation I produced a small hip flask of whisky, four plastic cups and called everyone to order. It was Christmas after all.

We'd reached the south wall of the churchyard. Del came back and sat on the wall, Tone went and sat two metres away from him. I poured out a shot for everyone and was proceeding to swig from the bottle when Sam elbowed me and suggested we should propose a toast. This was very ill-judged as I had only just removed my flask from my lips when the aforementioned elbow connected with mine and wobbled the bottle, spilling its contents down the front of my faux fur coat.

'Great,' I said after he had apologised. 'Now we smell of skunk,' I nodded at Tone, 'and whisky. The perfect fragrance for church.' At which point the donkey emitted a satisfied grunt and evacuated its bowels onto Bronson's feet.

Luckily, or unluckily, depending on your perspective, it being the time it was, we all had plenty of antibacterial wipes and hand sanitizer on us, which were duly offered to Bronson for cleaning purposes.

Of course when we reached the church we discovered it was closed. We'd forgotten places of worship were locked down too.

'Mmm,' said Bronson. 'Where then?'

This time it was Del who spoke up. 'Well, the pub's the hub isn't it? Shall we see if there's any activity down The Stars?'

No one had any better ideas so we crossed the road and entered the car park of our favourite local. Tone, who worked in their kitchen before he got furloughed, told us to come round to the side entrance. We followed him in a long, skinny, socially-distanced line with Del at the front, then Sam, then Bronson, then the donkey, then me. It must have looked quite odd.

After a few minutes of banging hard on the door, we heard the jiggling of keys on the other side and Lisa, the landlady, opened up.

She was indeed surprised to see us all standing there – complete with braying donkey and an incontinent baby doll – but got quite indignant when Tone asked if she knew anything about the furry ass. Although she may have misheard.

Once we'd cleared up that misunderstanding, Lisa did a bit of frowning, reiterated several times that the pub was not open, not even for takeaway drinks, and began to close the door.

For some reason Tone decided that this was the right moment to ask if it was possible to leave the donkey with her, so she could find out where it had come from.

Surprisingly Lisa wasn't into that idea and shook her head, insisting that there really was no space for it at The Seven Stars.

Sam turned to me. 'Did you hear that?' Then he gave the little doll a bit of an affectionate squeeze. For a moment, seeing him there holding the baby, my mind experienced a kind of timequake. A fleeting image of Sam at a window with a real baby in his arms whisked through my head. Strange, but also strangely nice. I cocked my head and smiled at him. Unexpectedly, something stirred within. I've never been a broody woman but I was overcome with the powerful urge to reach out and touch him. Maybe have a bit of a cuddle. Which of course was currently prohibited.

But I didn't. Instead I just said, 'What?'

'No room at the inn,' he replied with a nod towards the pub door.

'At Christmas too,' I said. 'Think I've heard of that happening somewhere before.'

He grinned and then took a few steps closer to the pub to listen in on the conversation with Lisa.

I didn't. Being at the back of the assembly I had a good view of our raggle-taggle group and noticed that the donkey had begun going a bit rogue. Its body was pointing across the car park. Both long ears twitched towards the woods that the car park bordered, as if it could hear something.

Curious.

I prodded Bronson and said, 'I think the donkey wants to get over there, to the forest. What do you reckon? Shall we let it go and see what happens?'

'Could do,' said Bronson and let the beast tug him across the backyard towards the break in the trees where the footpath opened up. There he unclipped the lead rope and we followed the beast through the bracken, past the scrawny skeletal nettles, the tawny rocks and evergreens sprouting from twisted tree roots.

The path curved south-west as we got deeper into the woods. The donkey carried on, taking a fork to the right.

'I think I know where it's going,' said Bronson.

I'd worked it out too. 'The Sitting Pool.'

'Want to be careful,' said Bronson.

I knew what he meant. It had a reputation. Allegedly, the site was the meeting-place of witches and fairies and was, apparently, charmed.

Local legend told of a fiddler who once went there to entertain some strange-looking folk. He sang and played and sat with them all night. In the morning when he went back to the village he found a century had gone past. I would have thought it was a load of old rubbish had it not been for some weird experience a few summers ago when I bumped into a couple of green protesters and completely lost my sense of time. Incidentally, when I say green protesters I'm not only referring to their ethical stance, but the grassy hue of their skin and earthy, elvish appearance. I'd seen them around since, but intermittently. They'd moved into a village not far away, though often travelled round the country campaigning against developments that encroached on natural habitats. They were good like that.

'Looks like he knows where he's going.' Bronson pointed at the donkey's tail disappearing behind a group of trunks. As we trailed it my own ears began to heat, tuning in to the faint sound of music and the tinkle of what softer-hearted people than me might think sounded like sleigh bells.

I passed under a low-hanging branch and came out into a ferny glade, a calm pool of water at its side.

The Sitting Pool.

The music was louder here.

I looked about and spotted, a few metres away, three people dressed in the sort of clothes that merged in with the background – blacks, greens, russets and greys. They appeared to be sitting quite comfortably on fallen trunks listening to a small but powerful speaker.

'Ah, there she is,' said a voice I recognised. 'Esmeralda! I told you she'd come back.'

Then Bronson cried, 'Karen! We've just been to the church.'

And I saw one of the three was our local vicar, who was still sporting her dog collar under her coat and smoking *another* suspicious-smelling cigarette.

'Oh hi, Bronson,' said the rev, completely unfazed. The Sitting Pool appeared to have worked its magic on her.

'Esmeralda!' said another female voice and one of the other two stood up and went to the donkey, rubbing its ears. 'Essie, old thing. Where did you go to?'

I realised at once that Karen's companions were the greenies, Ella and Elvin. Of course they were. Somehow I wasn't particularly surprised to find them here in the midst of the woods. In my mind, they always appeared rather fae-like, so it was reasonable to assume they wanted to be close to the pine trees, if not sitting on the top of one, on Christmas Day. Both of them looked completely at ease by the Sitting Pool, like they belonged to the place. My eye, however, was drawn to two things that didn't – a manger that stood beside the fallen logs, and beyond that a dappled cow tied up to a nearby willow tree.

'Hello Rosie,' said Elvin, calm as you like. 'Fancy seeing you here.'

'Hi,' I said to the three of them. 'Esmeralda? Is the donkey yours?'

Elvin nodded. 'We borrowed her from a sanctuary outside Chelmsford.' Then he looked at Karen, who was nodding and smoking with a blissed-out smile on her face.

'Ah,' she said. 'I wanted to do a nativity. There's been one in Adder's Fork for the past two hundred years. Elvin and Ella have helped me keep it going this year. So we can say it's an unbroken tradition. Of course, we've had to be a bit more creative.'

'But why didn't you do it at the church?' I asked.

'Not allowed. Needed somewhere more private.'

Ella smiled, 'And we wanted to give Karen her Christmas present,' she said.

Karen waved the cigarette at me. 'Helps with the rheumatism,' she said. 'Want some?'

I was holding out for the prosecco I'd seen Auntie Babs pop in the fridge, so I politely declined. Bronson however collected a neatly rolled cigarette. Then Ella offered me a can of G & T.

It was not like me to look a gift horse, or donkey, in the eye. So I accepted.

I think it was at this point that Karen insisted that Elvin put 'Mistletoe and Wine' on. The Greener scrolled through his phone and then selected the right track and, within minutes, Bronson was having a two-metre-distanced sort of waltz thing with Karen, while Elvin and Ella twisted each other in circles. Lacking a partner (story of my life) and devoid of the super-sexy Sam Stone, I decided to get on down with Esmeralda. Who did not move.

After that came a slew of questionable Christmas hits.

I think it was about the time we put on Slade's 'So Here it is Merry Christmas', and when I had finally managed to sit on Esmeralda's back without falling off, that we became aware of newcomers entering our midst.

'Bleedin' 'eck, this has gotta be the weirdest illegal rave ever,' said Tone, who was followed by Uncle Del, looking extremely annoyed, followed by Sam and the plastic doll, followed by a couple of young police officers.

Everyone hastily put out their smokes.

Tone, who was still laughing, took a photo and was told off by the shorter policeman.

'We were called to a disturbance at the Stars public house,' began the taller constable. He surveyed our odd group and then, noticing Karen's dog collar, addressed the rest to her, 'It is important that we verify the existence of a donkey.'

At which point I waved at them and pointed to the beast under my bum.

The next few minutes then exploded into something of a frenzy of 'explanation'. Elvin and Ella had to detail the appearance of the cow and donkey, Karen pleaded not guilty to the Covid Breach, I got off the donkey and, for want of anything better to do, took it over to the young policeman, who to be honest, was completely nonplussed by the whole situation.

After about ten minutes of this, during which order was not imposed, the officers seemed to weary. Or else they couldn't make sense of anything.

Or the Sitting Pool was doing its work.

Whatever, they sat down on Karen's log and accepted her offer of cigarettes.

'If you disperse peacefully,' said the older copper as Karen lit his fag, 'then we'll say no more.'

We were out of there before you could whisper 'Count your Christmas blessings.'

It was only later, as we trundled down Snakes Lane in the gathering twilight, that Sam relayed the events that had transpired at his end. Another miscommunication about the ass had occurred, which provoked a call from Lisa to the local constabulary. To clear up the facts of the matter it then became necessary to locate the actual donkey to which the suspects were referring, so they might ascertain the veracity of their story and avoid booking them as a public nuisance. Nobody wanted any extra paperwork on Christmas Day. The noticeable absense of any donkey in the car park, led to the despatch of a search party, which, after the passing of at least an hour, stumbled upon our not particularly legal nativity.

'Blimey,' I said. 'Well, I'm glad the Sitting Pool chilled them. Who knows what they might have done. We could have spent Christmas in the cells.'

'Stranger things have happened at sea,' said Bronson and put on his yellow sou'wester. 'Christmas '74, we were in the Bermuda Triangle …'

He was cut off by a ting from Sam's phone. The

curator fished out his mobile and then broke into a grin.

'Ah,' he said, 'a nativity for our times,' and held up the screen to us.

It was Tone's picture. Somehow, he'd managed to get us so it looked like Sam was leading me in on a donkey, while he carried the baby (doll) to the manger. Paying their respects to our holy trinity were a startled vicar, two green fairies, a man in a sou' wester, Uncle Del, and a couple of police officers.

'What a fine ass,' said Sam.

'Thanks very much,' I said and tried hard not to giggle.

The amber flecks in his eyes began to whirr and for a second there he looked very cheeky, but then there was a loud slam and we all turned towards the museum front door.

It was open. A cloud of smoke billowed out and thinned, revealing a bedraggled, less than sober Auntie Babs clutching a saucepan in a threatening manner.

'You lot better have a good excuse for this,' she said.

'Darling,' said Uncle Del. 'You wouldn't believe me if I told you.'

'Well you'll bleedin' make up for it. Get in there right now!' said Babs. 'Time for Drunk Twister.'

'At last,' said Sam and gave me a wink. 'Sanity. And who are we to turn down a lady's request?'

Emboldened by gin I gave his arm a squeeze and said, 'It's a dirty job but someone's got to do it.'

It was beginning to look like Christmas.

At last.

~~THIRTEENTH~~

The four housewives of the Apocalypse will not come on a Monday after the school run,

Nor will they come on Tuesday to put out the bins,

Or Wednesday to pay the milk bill.

The four housewives of the Apocalypse will not show up on Thursday afternoon for play dates.

They will not arrive on Friday after pizza night.

Nor on Saturday (weekly shop),

And never on a Sunday when the family is washing up (time to give mum a rest).

They will come in the night.

When least expected.

After the world has spun out of control and Pestilence, War, Famine and Death have done their best.

You will see them in the distance, on brown donkeys

from the sanctuary

With their shovels, seven long steps behind the horsemen:

Picking up discarded socks, beer cans, dirty plates, scooping the dung, spreading it across the roses.

They will come crouched and bent, with cramping wombs, trailing prams, biting tongues

Hot in their flushes

To soothe the dead, put them back to bed, sing sweet lullabies

Feed the famished, water plants, sort the weeds, ponder nutrition,

Administer Calpol, apply flannels to foreheads, take temperatures,

Change nappies, do the washing, walk the dogs, calm worries, allay frets, kiss and make up.

And after that they will go to work.

Justice. Peace. Fecundity. Birth.

Clearing up the mess of the world.

Quietly

In the night.

Before the alarm.

Before we rise.

ACKNOWLEDGEMENTS

What a year it has been. Indeed, 2020 had the biggest ever plot twist that (almost) no one saw coming. Everything, everything, has shifted and changed, and most of us are wondering if we will ever go back to 'normal' again. I felt it important, therefore, to make mention of the pandemic in some of my stories but not go overboard, taking the advice of my blimmin' amazing editor Jenny Parrott, who also this year emerged as a tower of strength and huge support on a personal level, too. A magical, top, top woman. There are others in the Oneworld Team who cannot go without recognition of their hard work and effort: Molly Scull, Margot Weale, Anne Bihan, Mark Rusher, Juliet Mabey, Novin Doostdar, Laura McFarlane and my sensitive copy editor, Francine Brody. Thanks must also go to my fearless agent,

Sandra Sawicka, for her counsel, common sense and encouragement.

Of course, lockdown has meant our worlds have shrunk with our geographical reach. But there are still friends who, though far away, have brought much-needed light into a very crazy time: Hugh Foster, Paddy Magrane, Olivia Edina Isaac-Henry, Steph Roche, Lisa Parrot, Kate Bradley – you are brilliant and luminous people.

My trouble bubble have done their best to keep spirits up, circulate dirty jokes and have also managed some bloody hilarious moments. Jo Farrugia, Curly Dan Newman, Josie Moore – you are nuts and I adore you. My old girls (not that old) didn't do too badly either: big kisses to Caroline Alexander, Lizzy Rant, Midge Jackson, Hobbit Mitchell, Jo Oats, Rachford Simnett, Tammy Peters, Sherry Bexfield, Rachel Lichtenstein, Elsa James and Colette and Andy Bailey, who have been solace to my soul and, again, kept me afloat when the dams were threatening to burst. If we move, we move together. Other incomparable, kind and generous local heroes include Peter and Sue Hall, Ray Morgan, Dave Farrugia, Jo and Brendan O' Hare, Steph and Robbie Stephenson. Nicola and Annabel Clarke were good Samaritans who rescued two stranded travelers in Farnham. Your kindness saved the day, thank you.

I must credit my beautiful friend, Jules Easlea, for suggesting I write about the Housewives of the Apocalypse. I hope you like what I came up with, babe. Now give me another.

Some epic supporters to acknowledge and appreciate for all their sterling work are Kayleigh Boyle from Snapping the Stiletto, Ciara Phipps from Southend Museums, the Essex Girls Liberation Front, Valina Bowman-Burns, Sarah Perry, and Ros Green of the Essex Book Festival. Keep fighting the good fight, my friends.

I have been inspired by various phenomenal short story writers, some of whom I can remember: Christopher Fowler, Susan Hill, Shirley Jackson, Cathi Unsworth, Roz Watkins. Deep gratitude goes out to all of you. However there are some who have slipped through my memory net. To those I must apologise and simultaneously express sincere thanks for their remarkable creativity.

And what can I say about Colin Scott? Words fail me. He is an absolute treasure. Cheers, Colin, for your wisdom and friendship. Without you the world would be a sadder place.

My family are similarly awesome. All the love

goes to Josie, Samuel, William, Arthur, Richard, Jess, Obie, Kit, Tony and Pauline Moore, Stella and Ernie Robinson, Joanne, Lee, Ronnie, Harry, Matty, John, Jess, Isla, Rye, Anais and Effie Sandell.

Last, but by no means least, the person who I have spent the year with, and who must therefore be praised to the high heavens – my very tolerant, able and talented Riley. Son, I could ask for no better.

ABOUT THE AUTHOR

Syd Moore is best known for her Essex Witch Museum Mysteries (*Strange Magic*, *Strange Sight*, *Strange Fascination*, *Strange Tombs* and *Strange Tricks*). The series was shortlisted for the Good Reader Holmes and Watson Award in 2018. She was shortlisted for the CWA Short Story Dagger in 2019 and 2020. Her debut screenplay, *Witch West*, which she developed from an original idea, has been optioned by Hidden Door Productions. Syd founded the Essex Girls Liberation Front and successfully got the term 'Essex girl' removed from the Oxford dictionary in 2020. Syd is also the author of *The Drowning Pool* and *Witch Hunt*. She lives in Essex.

For more Christmas chaos try
The Twelve Strange Days of Christmas

Shortlisted for the CWA Short Story Dagger 2019
'Spooky and sassy' *Sunday Times* Crime Club

On the first day of Christmas my dead love came to me…

Nothing says Christmas more than a good old-fashioned ghost story on a dark winter's night, so sit back and enjoy a little pinch of Yuletide mayhem.

These extraordinary tales, one for each day of Christmas, explore the odd, the peculiar and the downright chilling, from a strange encounter with an Icelandic Shaman, to a psychic policewoman, lively winged beasts and warnings from the recently departed.